HARLEM AND HAVANA 2

A HOOD LOVE STORY

MZ. KB

WANT TO BE A PART OF THE GRAND PENZ FAMILY?

To submit your manuscript to Grand Penz Publications, please send the first three chapters and synopsis to grandpenzpublications@gmail.com

HAVANA

As I stood in the parking garage screaming for help, I was trying to put pressure on Harlem's wounds, but I didn't know where to start. If I pressed too hard on the hole in his neck, it made the hole in his chest bleed more. Each second felt like a minute, and each minute like an hour, before someone finally came to help me.

A nurse who had just parked her car and was about to start her shift ran over to me and tried to help. She called a passerby to get and get a doctor. I was so relieved when a nurse came running out pushing a gurney with Dr. Grayson running behind her. I almost forgot about the strange incident where Harlem said he used to know her, but she seemed not to know who he was.

The only thing I can focus on right now is making sure Harlem is ok. Everything happened so quickly, but something about the shooter was so familiar. Even though he had a mask covering his face, I could've sworn I knew him from somewhere. Something about his eyes seemed all too familiar, like I've seen them before, but I can't place the face that they belong to.

Before the medical staff even had the chance to move Harlem, Kymani pulled up in his car.

"What the fuck happened, Havana? I just had a message from him not even ten minutes ago sayin'... Damn, Mya, is that really you? What the actual fuck is going on here?"

"I don't know who Mya is, but like I told your friend, you have me confused, sir. Could you please step aside and let us get him inside where we can try to help him?" Dr. Grayson instructed flatly before running alongside the gurney, still trying to treat Harlem.

"What the fuck happened?" Kymani turned back to me and asked.

"After Harlem saw Dr. Grayson, I could tell that something was playing on his mind. It's like he didn't even remember that I was there. He chased after her, calling her name, but she didn't seem to recognize him. He was still preoccupied when we walked into the parking garage. Both of us were looking at our phones. I was checking if my daddy had messaged me, and Harlem was sending a text. The next thing I knew, someone wearing a mask ran up and stopped in front of us, but before either of us knew what was happening, he was firing shots at Harlem. He didn't even have a chance to react. It all happened so quickly. It was awful, Kymani. He got hit so many times. I was trying to get him to look at me, but his eyes just kept closing. Oh my god, I just keep seeing it replaying in my head. He only came to pick me up. How could this have happened?" I tried to keep it together, but I couldn't help the tears from falling.

"I'ma call his pops and tell him what happened. You follow them and find out what's happening. I'll be right behind you." Ky instructed.

As I ran along the corridor behind the medical team helping Harlem, I could not get the entire incident out of my head. I kept replaying it over and over in my mind, searching for some sort of clue. Neither of us saw the shooter until it was too late. All I can do at this stage is pray that Harlem is ok.

The nurse told me to give Harlem's information at the registration desk and then take a seat in the waiting area, and someone would be out to update me as soon as they had any news. Thankfully, I knew some of his details due to our many late-night conversations. During my time staying with Harlem at his house, I felt like we connected when I stayed there. Although we haven't known each other for a long time, it feels like we have been around one another for years. There were so many nights that we sat up until sunrise talking about all kinds of stuff, so I know he had a girlfriend that died a few years back. He never told me her name, but I'm guessing it's Mya.

If she is Dr. Grayson, then I don't know what that would mean for us. As much as it would kill me to lose him before we even got started, I would step back if it meant he was happy. I can't think about all of that right now. I just need to know that Harlem is ok.

Kymani running back in startled me from my thoughts.

"His pops is on the way here now. Have they said anything?" he asked while taking the seat next to me.

"Not yet," I replied.

Kymani pulled out his phone and was about to make a call, but seeing the two detectives walking into the room, he put his phone back in his pocket.

"Hi, I'm Detective Ruiz, and this is my partner, Detective Hunter. We would like to ask you some questions about who shot your friend? Can you start by telling me what happened? Miss, I'm sorry I didn't get your name."

"We were walking to the car, and someone came out of

nowhere and fired at him. It all happened so quickly. I didn't see anything else. Sorry, I can't be of more help, but I was only just discharged, and I'm on strong pain medication. If I think of anything, I'll be sure to let you know," I replied, ignoring the fact that he asked for my name and smiling sweetly.

"Do you have any idea who would want to do this to Mr. Latrell? "

"No, I don't."

"Thank you for your time, ma'am," he replied before turning to Kymani. "If you know who did this, Mr. Young, you have to let us handle it. The video footage from the area has miraculously disappeared just that quickly. I don't suppose you know anything about that, do you?"

"Don't come in here accusing me of bullshit right now. Isn't it your job to investigate? Go fucking find the mother-fucker responsible for this before the streets do."

"We will be back to speak to Mr. Latrell once he regains consciousness, and if those tapes do happen to appear, I would appreciate them being sent to me. I'm warning you, Kymani, if I get one sniff of any kind of retaliation, then I will lock you up," the detective advised before they both walked out the way they came.

2

___

KYMANI

Just when I thought shit was finally gonna run smoothly for a minute, I woke up this morning to find out that three of the traps got hit and one of my couriers got jacked on the way back to the city. Luckily for me, I made her drop everything off with Dre, who took it all to the new safe house. In total, they got away with over eight stacks, which is nothing to us, but the violation was enough to sign their death warrant. I didn't even get the chance to tell Harlem about any of this before he got shot up. When I find out the motherfucker responsible for this, I swear on everything, I'ma fuck them all the way up. It seems like this is the year of people trying to violate us, and one thing for certain is that somebody will pay with their life. It's hunting season, and anyone is game right now.

I'm happy to see Havana is on the right page with talking to them pig motherfuckers. I peeped how she never answered what her name was, which was a smart move. We still don't know which one of these pigs her snake ass daddy has been working with. I don't even think Harlem has had a chance to speak to her properly yet.

"Yo, Ky, what the fuck happened? Where is my son?" Big H came storming into the waiting room, where I was sitting with Havana.

"Man... Harlem came to pick Havana up 'cuz she was getting discharged. When they made it out on their level to get the car, someone ran up and fired on him. He was in a pretty bad way. They haven't said anything else yet. But check this, three traps got hit this morning, and I was on my way here after getting a message from Harlem just before it happened. He said he saw Mya, and that she's not really dead. I thought he was tripping, but when I got here, she was the doctor working on him. It's like she doesn't even know me. Shit is fucked up, and we need to quickly get to the bottom of it. I got Tech to hack the system. He is currently going through every camera in the vicinity. He'll call me as soon as he knows anything."

"This bastard better pray the police find him before I do. I don't even know what to say about Mya. We were both there when the doctor said she didn't make it. If these motherfuckers lied and broke my son's heart, on gang, I'ma kill her fucking stuck-up ass parents!" Big H growled.

He looked to Havana as if he had just noticed her sitting there.

"Sorry, sweetheart, you must be Havana? I'm Harlem's dad, Big H. You've made quite an impression on my son. He's told me all about you. It's nice to meet you," he said, pulling Havana into a hug, the scared expression leaving her face instantly.

"Thank you, sir. Harlem had told me a lot about you. It's nice to meet you too."

"Can you tell me exactly what happened?"

Havana went on to explain to the big man exactly what

she told me. Hopefully, Tech will come back with something soon. Just as she finished her story, Mama Vee came rushing into the room.

"Where is my son? Someone better come out here and tell me what is going on!" she demanded, stopping a nurse who was walking past before noticing us sitting there.

"Nigga, why did I have to hear about this from Kymani? You couldn't call me your damn self? You're so fucking petty, Harlem. That is our son in there, and you didn't think to phone me? Selfish ass motherfucker!"

"Sit down, Valencia, and don't come at me with your bullshit today. Now is not the time or the fucking place for your antics. I'm not fucking with you right now, period. Don't say shit else to me with your lying ass. My son got shot. I'm not thinking about anyone but him."

"Fuck you, Harlem! Don't tell me shit, nigga," she sassed, but she still sat her ass down just like he told her to.

I know boss man is hella angry right now because in all my years of knowing him, I have never heard him yell at Mama Vee like that.

We sat around waiting in silence for what seemed like forever before someone came out to speak to us.

"Are you the family of Harlem Latrell?" the doctor asked.

"Yes, I'm his father."

"Your son suffered severe wounds to the head, chest, abdomen, and shoulder. We have managed to remove the bullets and the fragments in three of the wounds, but there is still some internal bleeding and damage to the liver. There is still part of a bullet lodged in his skull, but I can't risk operating on him further until he is more stable. The next forty-eight hours will be touch and go, and he is not out of danger yet, but he is a fighter. I'm sorry the news isn't better, but you will be able to see him soon. The nurse will come back and get you when you can go in."

"Thank you," Big H replied before the doctor walked away.

3

BIG H

I have the helicopter on standby 'cuz the second the doctor says Harlem is safe to move, I will be transporting his ass to somewhere more private, where he can be cared for properly. Until I catch the motherfucker responsible for this, I can't take the chance of them coming back to finish what they started. Just when I thought our problems were over, this happened. I don't care who I have to hurt or how many motherfuckers I have to lay down to make sure my family is all safe. I won't stop until I get at this motherfucker's head.

"Vee, I need you to get Brooklyn and Liberty. Take them both out to the lake house until I can get there. Sweetheart, I need you to phone Ashlee and tell her to come down here. You can drive with her. None of you can leave. It is important that y'all stay together. Kymani, make some calls and get security on this bitch 24/7. He is not to be left alone for one second. I don't care if the nigga's gotta shit. He better hold that until someone comes to take over his post."

I looked from one side of the room to the other, ensuring they all understood my orders. Yes, that's right, my orders.

My wife might like to run her mouth, but she knows who the fuck the boss is around here.

"Really, Harlem? And no disrespect, but we don't even know this little bitch. She could be the reason this all happened. After all, she knew he was coming here, so how do we know she didn't set it up?"

"I swear, I never—" Havana started, sounding scared, but I cut her off.

"She isn't involved. Plus, it doesn't matter if you know her now. You will get to fucking know her. She will be around for a long time, so I suggest you be nice to her. After all, Harlem is already pissed off with you after recent events, so you wouldn't want to do anything to push him further away," I warned my wife as I stared her down, daring her to fuck with me.

I felt bad, and I knew I had to tell them both about the other. I just didn't know what to say. I don't know what Harlem the chance had to tell Havana before he got shot.

Kymani's ringing phone made me break eye contact with my wife. I listened as he spoke to Tech. I was trying to hear what was being said on the other end of the phone, but the deep breaths my wife was now taking were muffling the sound. I shot her the death stare, but she just rolled her eyes at me like I didn't have the right to be pissed off with her.

"Tech found something, and he'll send it over in a minute. He saw a car speeding out of the parking garage just after Harlem got hit, so he's tracing the owner's name and address. I say we go pay this motherfucker a visit and see what's good."

"You can go back and see him now." Kymani was cut off by the nurse who came into the waiting room.

One by one, we walked into the room to see Harlem. Just seeing him laid out on the bed with tubes and wires everywhere like that hurt my soul. My kids are my world and seeing any of them hurt is too much for me, but this was another level of pain. When I get my hands on the motherfucker responsible, I swear on everything I love, I will kill them.

Havana went to one side of his bed and Vee on the other. Looking at them both together, I could see the resemblances. It was only then that I realized just how alike they were. It was only a matter of time before Vee realized Havana was her daughter.

"There is something I need to tell you both."

"I don't want to hear anything you have to say right now. Just find the person responsible for this and make them pay. I'm going to get the kids. I take it you'll give *her* the address?" Vee said before kissing Harlem on his head and walking out without giving me a second glance.

"That woman is so damn hard-headed. Kymani, follow her, please, and make sure she is safe. If I go after her, I might just break my foot off in her ass."

"You got it," he replied with a chuckle.

I looked at Havana.

"I'm not sure what Harlem told you before all this happened, and I don't even really know how to say this. I know he wanted to speak to you because some information has come to light about your biological mother. I have to keep it one hundred with you with everything going on, now more than ever. My wife is your mother. She had a relationship with your dad years ago. He told her you died, and she never told me about it. That is why we're having a disagreement right now. I promise you it isn't always like this. I am pissed off that she wasn't honest with me, but I know it is because losing you broke her heart, and she could never bring herself to speak on it. If we had known about you, I swear I would've found you before now. This is not the way I wanted you to find out, but I had to tell you before I sent y'all off to stay together. Please don't hate her. She honestly believed that you had died. She's not always like she was today. She is just mad and hurt right now. I'm going to speak to her when I leave here and tell her too. I want you to go with Ashlee to the lake house, and as soon as Harlem is stable enough, I am moving him there until we find out who did this. He will kill me if anything happens to you," I just blurted it out.

4

———

HAVANA

Right now, my mind is all over the place. I can't even begin to process what has transpired in the seventy-two hours. My entire life is a mess right now, and I feel like I'm losing all control. My daddy has disappeared and is not answering his phone, so he can't answer any questions I have. Right about now, all I want is to go home, curl up in my bed and get so high that I forget any of this even happened.

"I'm not sure what to even say right now, and I don't want to sound rude, but this shit is fucked up. I need some time to process everything; I think I should just go home."

"I can't let you do that, not to your house on your own. The lake house is big enough that you won't have to see anyone if you don't want to. I can give you tonight, but tomorrow I will have to tell my wife the truth," Big H replied.

"Ashlee is on her way here to get you," Kymani informed me as he walked back into the room before he turned to Big H.

"I've got an address. The car is registered to some bitch named Shania that Harlem used to fuck with. Obviously, the beat down her ass got from Miss Havana here hurt her feelings. Let's swing by her crib and find out who has been driving her car and what her involvement is in all of this. It makes sense. She knows where all the traps are located 'cuz she worked for us. The security just arrived. They are parking the car, so they'll be here in a minute."

Ashlee walked in behind who I can only assume is the security. As soon as she saw me, she ran to me and hugged me tightly. As soon as I fell into her embrace, the tears I had been holding back began to fall. No matter how many times I tried to compose myself, all I could do was cry on the shoulder of my best friend.

"It's ok, friend."

"Nothing is ok, Ashlee. I need to get out of here," I replied, straightening myself up and walking over to Harlem.

I placed a soft kiss on his head and reassured him I would be back soon. The conversation we had the other night played over in my mind, and the call I can hear is Harlem telling me I need to get on my grown woman shit. It is time I put on my big girl panties. I am the daughter of a fucking legend, and it's time I acted like it. My daddy raised me to be smarter than I have been acting these last few months, and it's time to wake the fuck up and boss the fuck up. I am the daughter of a fucking legend and it's time I acted like it.

Looking at Big H and Kymani, I started to speak. "I am going with Ashlee. I need a change of clothes and to pack a bag. Harlem had all of my stuff moved before this happened, but Ashlee has the things I'll need at her house. We're going back there, and then I'm going to come back and spend some time with Harlem, and then I'll go to the lake house."

"You can't go alone. I'll have someone follow you," Kymani informed me.

Big H walked toward me and pulled me into a hug before whispering in my ear, "I'm sorry that I had to tell you like that, but you needed to know. Please be careful and don't leave your security."

I walked out of the hospital with Ashlee. Big H and Kymani were following us to the car and then going to find this bitch from the block party. I wish I could go with them. I'd do more than beat her ass this time.

The second we got into the car, I looked over at Ashlee.

"Tell me you have some weed?" I quizzed.

"Girl, I have a blunt in my purse, but there is more at my crib. Are you ready to tell me what happened?"

Grabbing Ashlee's Dior purse, I went inside and found the blunt and a lighter. I lit the tip and took a few good pulls to try to calm my nerves before I started to speak.

"This has got to be the most fucked-up week of my life. First, I find out that Ameena has been fucking Tip behind my back, which is just disgusting. Then I find out that she is not even my mom, which is just fucked up. My dad has disappeared, and now Harlem's dad just told me that his wife is my mom. Oh, fuck! Fuck! Fuck! Does that mean that Harlem is my brother? I swear I want to die right now."

"Girl, that man is not your brother. Mama Vee is not his biological mom. She is his stepmom. He went to live with his dad a few years back, and they grew close. Can't nobody tell him that's not his mama, though, but you have nothing to worry about," Ashlee reassured, trying not to laugh.

"It's not funny, Ashlee!"

"The way I see it, at least you don't have to put up with Ameena the ice bitch anymore. Let her and that no-good ass nigga Tip rot in hell together. You know he was never good enough for you, anyway. That entire situation opened your eyes to a lot of fucked up shit, but at least you're rid of both now. Your *man* made sure of that. He has made sure neither of them will ever hurt you again. And girl, fuck your daddy. He lied to you all these years and left you without your real mom, and for what? I don't know what happened with him and Mama Vee, but she is nice. She is a much better mom than Ameena ever was. Your daddy is fucked up for that. Leave his crazy ass where the fuck he's at right now. I'm sure he'll be back in a few months, begging you to talk to him. When you see what was in his safe, you'll feel better. You're a rich bitch in your own right. You don't need any of them. From now on, you should only surround yourself with people who are real and those who treat you right."

I can always trust my best friend to put shit into perspective for me, even if it is in her own crazy way.

We both sat quietly in our thoughts for the rest of the drive back to Ashlee's crib. The second we got inside the house, Ashlee pulled me into her guest bedroom and pulled a bag out from under the bed.

"Check this out," she said, pulling the bag open.

"Holy shit! All of this came out of my daddy's safe?" I asked, almost not believing my eyes.

"Yes, girl! I told you! Listen, I've got some calls to make, so I'll meet you downstairs once you've showered and changed."."

I SPENT the next hour going through the manilla folders that were inside the safe. There were deeds to eight different properties throughout the city, one for our old house back in Atlanta and two in New York. There was paperwork for the five different businesses that he owned. Two were hair salons, and then there was a restaurant, a bar, and a night-club. Inside a folder, there was a copy of my daddy's will and my original birth certificate, naming Valencia Carter as my mother. The last folder I got to contained details of bank accounts. There were two in my name and one for each of my brothers. When I looked at the balance of each of the accounts, I thought I would pass out. My brothers each have three million dollars. One of my accounts also had the same. However, the last account I looked at has over fifty million dollars in it. There must be some kind of mistake, I know my daddy is rich, but this is a different level of rich. An envelope was attached to the back of the folder. Opening it, I pulled out a letter and started to read.

My Darling Heaven,

If you are reading this, then it means that something has happened to me, and I am sorry that I am not there with you right now.

You are my world. Ever since the day I found out that your mom was pregnant, everything I have ever done was so you could have the best life possible, and I hope when you look back at your life, your memories are filled with nothing but love. Hold on to that feeling, baby, because what I am about to tell you may change how you feel about me for the rest of your life.

Your mom's name is Valencia Carter. I am sorry I never told you before, but Ameena is not your real mom. Before you were born, your grandfather made me marry Ameena, but I never loved her, not really. Your mom was the love of my life, but I hurt her in the worst possible way. I took you and told her you died. At the time, I thought it was the best thing for everybody, but I was being selfish. Coming up to your first birthday, I went back to find her and tell her the truth, but she had moved. I spent weeks looking for her, but I couldn't find her anywhere. Social media was not around in those days, so I hired someone to find her, but they came up with nothing. I decided to take you back home to Ameena and continue raising you at home with your brothers.

I know nothing will ever make up for the betrayal that you're probably feeling right now, but I have left everything I own to you. All my worldly possessions are yours. The houses, the cars, the money, everything is yours. Antonio Junior and Alonso will get everything their mother has when she dies and the bank accounts I left for them, as well as the street business in Atlanta. They can have free reign over all that side of things, as it is no life for my princess to be involved in.

I am so sorry for not being a better man, but the love I have for you will always be the same. You are my world, my every-thing, my heaven on earth.

I love you and always will.

-Daddy

BY THE TIME I got to the end of the letter, I couldn't help but let the tears fall. I went into the bathroom and put the playlist on my phone before stripping off and getting in the shower. I stood under the hot water, letting it rain down on me, and cried silently. The emotions I had running through my body were overwhelming, and it was difficult to focus on anything else, but Harlem needed me, so it was time to fix myself up and go and make sure my man was ok.

THIRTY MINUTES LATER, I walked back into the bedroom to find some clothes. I dressed down in a simple black Gucci tracksuit and my black Balenciaga sneakers with the white sole. I put my hair up in a messy bun and put some make-up on. I walked downstairs to find Ashlee, who was putting some food onto plates in the kitchen.

"I'm starving! What are you cooking?" I quizzed as I joined her at the stove.

"Bitch, you're funny! You know I'm not cooking anything. I just ordered some food to be delivered. Here, take this while I go outside and give DJ some food," she said as she handed me two plates loaded with chicken, rice, and salad.

We sat at the breakfast bar in the kitchen, and I wasted no time tucking into the food in front of me. This is the best-tasting meal I have had in days. That hospital food had no flavor. It's like they don't know what seasoning is in that place, real white people's food.

"I need to get back to the hospital and find out what is happening with Harlem. Let's finish this food and get going," I said between mouthfuls.

"You need to take care of yourself too, Havana. You should be resting. Remember, you just came out of hospital yourself."

"Yes, I will, but I need to make sure he is ok. You can just drop me off, and I promise I will call you to pick me up when I'm ready. I can't go and sit in that lake house with Vee, knowing that she is my mom. I just need a little time to get my head around it all. I'll be fine, friend, I swear."

WHEN WE FINALLY MADE IT back to the hospital an hour later, I couldn't wait to get inside and see Harlem. The security came out to meet me and take me back to the hospital. As I made my way up to his room, I remembered my phone was in my purse on silent still. Pulling it out, I checked my messages as I waited for the elevator to come. As soon as it stopped, I stepped in and pressed the button while reading the messages on my phone. Seeing one from Harlem, I got my hopes up until I realized it was from his dad on his phone. He said he had moved Harlem to the lake house, and I should meet them there. Typical. I just got all the way here, and I missed them by ten fucking minutes. I waited for the elevator to go up and back down again while typing a message to Ashlee, asking her to come back and get me.

I wasn't even paying attention to my surroundings, so I didn't realize that it was just myself and the security left on the elevator.

"Harlem has been moved. How didn't you know that?" I asked, feeling irritated as fuck with this dumb ass.

I was still watching my screen for the three little dots signaling Ashlee was typing a reply when he grabbed me from behind, and something was put over my mouth and nose. Whatever it was made me feel sick. The smell was awful, and within seconds I could feel myself losing control of my legs and almost falling before being picked up and put over the man's shoulder. The next thing I knew, everything was black.

5

KYMANI

The second the others left the hospital, Big H made a few calls and got Harlem moved in a helicopter up to the lake house. He sent security there to watch over the house and the rest of the family while we went over the address that I'd been given for Shania.

Whoever this nigga is that she be fucking with really had upgraded her broke ass and taken her out of the hood and had her holed up in a nice little suburb with some cute houses. I had to laugh thinking of Shania and her ratchet ass friends fucking up this nice peaceful-looking street. I just bet the people who live here already hate her ass.

We quietly got out of the car and walked straight up to the door. I tried the door handle before knocking, and I was surprised to see the door open. I had to laugh again because people were so fucking predictable. This bitch must've thought she was untouchable. Even in the hood, her door was never locked. We both walked in with our straps raised and closed the door, quietly locking it behind us.

I could hear someone moving around at the back of the house, so we headed into the kitchen to find Shania cooking. The second she saw us, she dropped the pan she was holding, and the hot oil splashed all up her bare legs. She let out a cry, but I quickly hit her over the head with the butt of my gun, and she dropped to the floor. I pulled her limp body into a chair, so I could tie her up and then gagged her to stop her from screaming when she woke up.

Big H told me to go and check the rest of the house to make sure there wasn't anyone else here. I went looking around the house, but Shania was here alone. When I walked into the master bedroom, I saw a phone lit up on the side. I grabbed it and noticed a missed call from two minutes ago from *Baby*. I put the phone in my pocket and turned to leave when I noticed a couple of duffle bags on the floor. Looking inside them, I was shocked to see that one was full of guns and ammo, the other was full of money. I picked up both bags and took them back downstairs with me.

"Yo boss man, look what the fuck was lying on the floor upstairs," I said as I opened the bags in front of him. Big H shook his head as he stood up and slapped Shania, making her wake the fuck up with a shock.

"Hmmm mmmm mmm..." She tried to speak, but all that could be heard were muffled sounds behind the gag over her mouth.

"I am going to take the gag off, but if you scream, I'll shoot you. Ok?" Big H asked her, and she nodded her head up and down.

He moved forward to remove the gag but stopped before speaking again. "You have one chance to tell us the truth, or this will not end well for you, Shania," he said before moving forward again, this time removing the gag from her mouth.

"What do you want?" she asked, clearly scared.

"Who are you working with?" he asked, just as the phone in my pocket started ringing again. I pulled it out and looked at the screen. There was the name *Baby* again.

"Who is this?" I asked, shoving the screen in her face.

"That's my man, A.J..," she answered. "He is on his way home. He will be here any second. You don't want him to find you here."

"Do you think I give a fuck about some little nigga? Girl, I was in these streets before your daddy even knew how to bust his nut, so shut the fuck up. I want answers, and if you don't tell me what the fuck I want to hear, then you'll be a dead bitch before your little boyfriend makes it through that door. Don't fucking play with me!" Big H angrily spat before grabbing Shania by the hair and making her look at him. "Why did that little nigga shoot my fucking son and rob my traps? Were you that desperate after Harlem stopped fucking with you that you wanted some type of payback or some shit?" I asked her.

"He shot Harlem. No, no, no! He was just supposed to help me hit a few of the traps. I didn't want anyone getting hurt, especially not Harlem. Ky, you know I love him, I could never... I just needed some money. Harlem just stopped fucking with me and told everyone I wasn't allowed to work. I couldn't earn any money, and I had bills to pay. I never even showed him where the main traps were, only a few smaller ones. I just needed a bit of money to get by until I could find a job or try to convince Harlem to let me come back to work," she blurted.

"My fucking son is lying in a hospital bed, and we don't know if he is even going to make it and you're sitting there telling me all of this was over some fucking money. Who the fuck is this A.J., and where can I find him?"

"He's just someone I met. He started talking to me a few

months ago. He approached me at the store when I was with my girls and asked if he could take me out. We've been rocking since then," she replied.

"Put this bitch in the trunk, and we'll take her to the warehouse. I'll make some calls and get someone to sit on the house until he gets back."

"Please, I'll tell you everything."

"Speak. You have sixty seconds before I blow your fucking wig back, so stop playing with me."

"His name is Antonio. He and his brother Alonso have been robbing the traps to get back at y'all. He said years ago, the city belonged to his father, and you set him up so you could take over. He hates Harlem and thinks he killed his mom. I didn't know that he shot him, though. He just said he was going to take everything he loved."

"Fucking Yayo!" Big H spat. "Put this bitch in the trunk, and we'll take her to the warehouse. She can't be fucking trusted to live. Look how easily she just gave up her man."

I'll make some calls and get someone to come and sit on the house until this little prick reappears.

"If this is linked to Yayo, then what are we going to do with Havana? How do we know she's not involved?" I hated to be the one to ask the questions, but someone had to.

6

ASHLEE

When we pulled up outside the hospital, the security came out to meet Havana. The minute she stepped out of my car, I called out for Siri to phone Kymani, but typically, my battery was dead. I pulled into a parking lot to plug my phone into the charger so I could phone and check in with my man. I just know he is feeling it with everything going on. Harlem is more than his best friend. They are brothers, and one without the other makes no sense. I've been praying for him, and I hope he has a quick recovery. Kymani and Big H will make the streets bleed behind Harlem, and Havana will go out of her mind. She feels like he is all she has left now, and I must admit I'm shocked by how they have fallen so hard for each other in such a short amount of time. Still, I'm happy for them, and secretly I've been trying to set them up for the longest.

The second my phone powered back on, messages started coming in from Kymani and my mom. I opened Ky's message, and it said that they were moving Harlem out of the hospital and that I was to go straight up to the lake house with Havana. I started the car, turned around, and headed out of the parking lot and back toward the hospital, phoning Kymani as I did so.

"Hey, baby. You, ok?" he asked as soon as he answered the phone.

"Yea, I'm ok. I just dropped Havana back at the hospital before I saw your message as my phone died. I've just got back to where I dropped her, so hopefully, she'll be out in a minute. Did Harlem wake up?"

"Not yet he didn't, but we didn't feel safe with him there, so we brought him up to the lake. Hurry and get here. Daddy needs some pussy."

"Boy, even with everything going on, all you think about is pussy. You a trip for real, baby, but I love your freaky ass. As soon as Havana gets her ass back out here, I'll be on the way."

We spoke for a few more minutes before I told him to get off the phone so I could phone Havana and see where the fuck she was.

I sat outside the hospital for almost thirty minutes trying to phone Havana, but I kept getting her voicemail. After leaving her a message telling her to wait at the car, I went inside to try to find her, but none of the nurses who were earlier looking after Harlem had seen her. I got back into the car and phoned Ky back again.

"She isn't here. I went inside, but the nurses hadn't seen her, and there was no answer on her phone. I don't know where she has gone, but it makes no sense that she would just disappear when all she wants is to see Harlem. I watched her walk into the building."

"Where the fuck was y'all security? I told that nigga don't let either of y'all leave his sight."

"He waited for the other security to come and meet her, and then he got back in the car and followed me," I said.

"What other security? There ain't no one else there. I'ma phone him now, I don't know who the fuck he gave her to, but someone is going to fucking pay for this. Just bring your ass on up to the lake now, Ashlee. Damn, as if we don't get enough to deal with right now. I'll talk to you when you get here. Just hurry. Don't stop anywhere. Just drive straight here!" he growled before ending the call on my ass.

Ky is lucky I'm not in the mood for bullshit today, or we would have a problem, but he is right. We have enough to deal with outside of arguing. I don't know where the fuck Havana got to, but I hope she turns up soon. One thing for certain is that if Harlem wakes up and Havana isn't there, then he won't be happy. I don't know where she could've gone unless she went back to her house, but she didn't mention anything to me.

The drive to Big H's Lake house was a little over an hour, so I put my music on and started to drive. My mind was all over the place. It didn't matter how loud I sang along to the lyrics of the song that was playing. I was really worried about what Kymani would do when he found out who shot Harlem. I'm scared that I'd lose him. I hated how he was still in the streets, but he promised me that he would leave it all alone in a few years so we could settle down. I want to get married and have his babies now, but we agreed to wait until I am twenty-five. Kymani is my entire world. My life revolves around him. Outside of our relationship, I only really have my mama and Havana. I don't know what I would do if something happened to him.

I must've tried Havana's phone at least another thirty

times since leaving the hospital but still nothing. At this point, I'm getting more worried about her. It's not like her not to answer her phone for me. We still don't know who shot Harlem, and I'm scared that the same person has done something to Havana.

PULLING up at the lake house, four men were outside carrying AKs. One of them walked up to my car and asked my name. I told him who I was just as Kymani appeared at the front door. I parked my car and ran into my man's arms.

"I'm worried that whoever did this to Harlem has done something to Havana. It makes no sense that she would just disappear, not without knowing that Harlem is ok."

"How well do you know Havana? Do you think she could somehow be involved?" he asked.

"No, she would never do anything like this. Havana really cares for Harlem. Why would she want to hurt him?"

"What about her brothers? How well do you know them?"

"I've met them, but I don't know them. Havana doesn't get along with her brothers. She thinks they are both idiots. A.J. is the oldest. He seemed friendly enough when I met him, but Alonso is rude, and he seems a bit dumb. Why are you asking me all these questions?"

"We think they had something to do with Harlem getting shot, and we're trying to work out if Havana is involved," Big H stated as he walked outside to where we were standing.

7

———

HAVANA

When I woke up, I was lying on a bed in a small bedroom. The window was boarded up from the outside, only letting small amounts of light through the gaps in the wood. Looking around, the only thing in the room was the bed and a TV on the wall. I stood up and walked toward the door. I tried opening it, but it was locked. I went to the other door, and that one opened into a small bathroom. There was a bottle of water next to the bed, which I greedily picked up and gulped down. The TV turned on made me jump as it lit up the room, and there was a woman's face on the screen.

"I suggest you get comfortable, Havana. You're not going anywhere for a while. You're safe now. You're with family. Just relax," the woman voiced through the screen.

"I don't know who you are, but you're not my family. Just let me go!"

"I'll give you some time to adjust to your new surroundings, and then we will talk properly, but just take my advice and do as you are told and make this easier on yourself."

Before I even got the chance to respond, the TV went

blank, and I was left alone again. I sat in the room with nothing to do but think. I don't know who she is, and I'm pretty sure I've never even seen her before, so I don't know what she could want with me. I just hope this isn't linked to Harlem getting shot, but the way my life has been going recently, you can bet your bottom dollar that it is.

Just a few months ago, my life was pretty much perfect. I had everything a girl of my age could want, and now I have nothing left. I wish I'd never even met Tip. He was the start of all my problems, and everything has been moving so fast that I haven't even started to process what my life has become. I know Tip and Ameena were dead, but I don't know where my daddy was. Just reading the letter that he left me in his safe, I was starting to think he's gone too. I haven't seen or heard anything from A.J. or Alonso, so I don't even know if they know what has happened to Ameena. I've never been close to either of them, but they're my big brothers, and all I have left, so I thought they would've at least phoned me when they realized something was wrong at home.

I feel so alone, like the only people left in my world are Ashlee and Harlem, and I don't even know if he'll want to know me if he wakes up — *when* Harlem wakes up, when not if. I must keep telling myself he will be ok because I can't stand the thought of anything else happening to him. Since he met me, there has been nothing but drama, so I couldn't blame him if he is done with me. The only thing that I have going in my favor is that I have enough money to live.

The sound of the bedroom door being unlocked snapped me out of my thoughts. I was so happy when I saw my brother Alonso walk in.

"Alonso, thank god! How did you know I was here?" I

said, jumping up to greet my big brother but being met with a slap so hard it knocked me off my feet.

"Get the fuck up, Havana!" he yelled while grabbing me by my hair and dragging me down the flight of stairs to the ground floor of the house.

Sitting in the other chair was my oldest brother, A.J., the guy from the elevator, and the same woman that had earlier appeared on the television screen.

"Sit down, Havana!" A.J. ordered. I sat in the seat he had motioned me toward.

"A.J., what is going on, and why the fuck did this asshole just slap me?"

"You have some explaining to do. Why were you with the nigga that killed mama?"

"He didn't kill her," I defended, just to be hit with another slap to the side of my head by Alonso.

"Don't take me for a fucking idiot, Havana. Pops might buy that innocent shit you be acting like, but I don't. After his old man got locked down, Pops had us rob some of this motherfucker's traps. Now his dad is out of jail, and both mom and dad have vanished. Don't you think that is a bit suspicious? And then I find out that my little sister is fucking with the enemy. I watched back the recording from the camera that overlooks the driveway, and I saw Harlem take mama out of the house, so if he didn't kill her, then where the fuck is she?"

"She had me beaten and raped. She was sleeping with my boyfriend behind my back and set up the whole thing to try to destroy me because she was jealous of my relationship with daddy. It was him who had her killed, not Harlem. Harlem brought her to the hospital to give me the answers I deserved, but she left with daddy. Harlem did not kill her. I can't believe you shot him, and you didn't even have the facts!"

"Fuck all of that. I don't believe you. You would say anything to protect your little boyfriend, but you couldn't protect him from the bullets I pumped into him. How could you lie about our mom like that?"

"She's not my mom. She's your mom, but not mine. Daddy told me the truth, and he said Ameena wasn't my mother. I am the child of him and another woman. That is why she always treated me differently from you boys. She never liked me, and don't pretend you didn't notice."

"You're lying. You never got along with her. You constantly fought her on everything, and you always disrespected her, which is why she didn't like you, not because you weren't her child," Alonso butted in.

"If you don't believe me, I have proof. I have a letter from daddy that explains everything. He told me to go into the safe and inside were some documents and a letter. We each have a bank account with money just in case anything ever happened to either of them. He said I would get my share of his legitimate businesses, but all the street shit and everything belonging to Ameena would be split between you both. She never liked me, but she raised me so that you would both have the life you were born into. She knew if she refused, then daddy would leave her."

"I want to see the letter and the details to the bank accounts," Alonso announced.

"I want answers, and only Harlem and that motherfucking Big H can answer them," A.J. added.

The woman was saying something under her breath. I couldn't quite hear what she was saying, but it was clear she had some sort of issue with them just by the look on her face.

"Well, then it was a bit fucking stupid to shoot him then, wasn't it?" I commented sarcastically before looking at the woman sitting opposite me. "And who the fuck are they?"

"This is D, she's been helping us, and this is her son Harvey. They have their own issues with Big H and Harlem. They'll be taking care of you until I get you moved. I'm sending you back to Atlanta to live after I finally get rid of Harlem and Big H. Take her back to her room, Alonso."

"What the fuck do you mean? I'm not going to Atlanta, and you can't kill Harlem. He's done nothing to you! You must let me go, A.J.! Please! I'm your sister. How could you do this to me?"

Before I could even put up a fight, Alonso punched me in the jaw and dragged me back upstairs, locking me in the bedroom again.

8

A. J

Yeah, ok, so y'all already think I'm the bad guy, so y'all already hating on a nigga. However, you don't know my side of the story.

My father was the king of this city until motherfucking Big H set him up so he could take over. We just came back here to take back what was rightfully ours. Ever since I could remember, my dad told me stories about his days running the streets of Chicago, and by the time I reached my thirteenth birthday, I was already being trained to take over my family's legacy.

It was in my bloodline to be involved in the sale of drugs. My grandfathers for generations have owned coca and heroine fields in Cuba and have sold their product in cities in every damn state. My grandfather told me that as the eldest son of the eldest son, they would all belong to me one day.

When we came back here, my dad was supposed to be making moves to take over while my brother and I started putting a crew together. For years, I watched this nigga rolling around the city in his flash cars, dripping in ice without a care in the world as if he couldn't be touched. I got sick of waiting for my dad to do anything, so I formulated a plan. I would hit them where it hurt and run up on all their blocks and traps one by one. I met this crackhead named D. She knew Big H and was happy to feed me information if I fed her habit. She and her son Harvey have their own issues with Harlem and Big H. From what Harvey has been telling me, Harlem ruined his life, and they want to see him fall. I don't care what their issue is, but I'll keep them both around if they can be of use to me.

After the first trap was hit, these motherfuckers switched up the entire operation, so I knew I needed another way in. That's where Shania came in. When I approached her, I already knew that she worked for Harlem, so she would be able to give me the information I needed. She was salty as fuck about this little nigga having a new girl, so she was an easy target. All I had to do was chuck a bit of money around and make her feel like she was special. The second I dropped that dick off in her, she was putty in my hands.

What I didn't know was that the new girlfriend she was complaining about was my fucking sister. Imagine my surprise when Havana walked out of the hospital with him, but I didn't care. I wasn't about to her get in my way. I knew I couldn't hurt her, or my dad would kill me, so I had to make sure my aim was on point.

Ever since I can remember, Havana has always been my pop's favorite child. It's more than just the fact that she is his only daughter. They had a bond like no other, and both Alonso and I hated her for it. Havana took up every single spare minute he had, and he rarely showed my brother or me any attention unless it was to teach us the family business.

My grandfather was the best role model I had, being

that my father spent so much time away from home. He had to travel to different cities and check the running of the operation. That's what he led us to believe, but in all reality, I know he was with different bitches in each city. I hated the way he treated my mom, but in a way, it was her fault for allowing it. My father has always been my mother's biggest weakness. He was like a drug she was addicted to. She just couldn't let go. It didn't matter how many times he stepped out on their relationship or how many times he would openly disrespect her. She would always stay.

On the outside looking in, you would think she only stayed for the money and my father's lifestyle. In truth, my mom had money in her own right. Her father left her millions when he died, which she has squared away for a rainy day. But no, the thing with her is that she saw divorce as a failure and refused to lose face. It's as if she was saying it was ok for him to cheat if he never divorced her.

I grew up in a fucked-up family, but I knew I wouldn't be like them. I would marry for love, not because my parents told me this is who I would be with.

Anyway, back to what's important. When I saw Havana with Harlem walking out of the hospital, I knew I had to get her away from those people. No way was my sister gonna fuck around with the enemy. The problem with Havana is that she has been raised in a bubble. My father is so over-protective of her, and she has always been sheltered from the life we were born into. She is young, naïve, and easily fooled. I just know he is using her to get to us. He must've worked out that we were responsible for hitting his traps and jacking his courier. It doesn't matter now because he won't be waking up from the shots that I pumped into him. As soon as I feel it is safe to do so, I'm moving Havana back to Atlanta to live with our uncle, my father's younger brother.

I sent my Harvey to pose as security and grab Havana from the hospital, but when he got there, she had already left. I told him to hang around for a while 'cuz I was sure she would be back. If that nigga Harlem meant anything to her, she is guaranteed to be back to visit his ass.

Alonso thinks Havana was playing us, but I swear that motherfucker be doing too much coke to even think straight. I let him get away with hitting her today to scare her, but I'm not down with how he is acting. I warned him that if he puts another hand on her, I'll knock his ass out and break his nose so he can't sniff shit.

Ever since I got back from shooting that little bitch Harlem, D has been acting really salty with me.

"Yo, what is your problem? You know the plan," I asked her.

"You weren't supposed to hurt Harlem, just Big H," she replied with an attitude.

"What's it to you? We are taking over, and I don't care who has to get hit for these motherfuckers to get the message. There's a new boss in town, and they need to know."

"Yea, yea, whatever nigga," she replied before walking off into the other room.

9

VEE

Leaving the hospital, I made my way to pick up Brooklyn and Liberty. I knew neither one of them would be happy about being dragged away from their lives and be made to stay at the lake house with us, but right now, it's just tough shit. I am not in the mood to argue. I warned them the second I delivered the news. Liberty just looked at me with contempt in her eyes, and I just knew she would be the one to argue with me. My son Brooklyn was so laid back that nothing bothered him, and I knew the only thing he would be concerned about was that his girlfriend Larissa could come with us. The two of them are glued at the hip these days, so I was expecting the question and had already decided that if that's what it took to keep him safe, she could come with us. I know my husband won't be happy, but I don't give a fuck right now.

Big H has been walking around here like he's the only one with the right to be pissed off. Last I checked, it was him sitting with some thot bitch all over him at Harlem's house, not me, and it was him who has been fucking that lawyer bitch. Yes, I know I fucked up, but him doing what he did out of spite is just as bad. I have lied, but I have never stepped out on our marriage but judging by the text message exchange on his burner phone, he was letting that bitch suck and fuck on him while he was in jail. That is a disrespect I wouldn't normally dream of tolerating, but with the truth coming out about Heaven the way it did, I don't have a leg to stand on with my argument. My daddy always used to tell me, *"You can't be wrong and strong."* And I knew I was in the wrong this time. I still deserve an explanation and being that my husband doesn't want to give it to me, I guess I will have to find this Imani bitch and see what she has to say.

I've been spending all my spare time online trying to find Heaven, but I'm not getting anywhere. I've searched all over Facebook and Instagram, but I'm coming up short each time. I've been forced to hire a private detective to try to find her. Imani, on the other hand, was much easier to locate. I have managed to find her office address and her home address. I'm just waiting for my chance to get away from the house with no security, and you can believe this bitch will be seeing me. She clearly doesn't care about her security because she has all her information on display for anyone looking for it. For such an intelligent woman, she is dumb as fuck.

Hearing the helicopter overhead made me look outside. I was shocked to see it was landing right in the yard of our lake house. I pulled out my phone to call my husband and realized that I had three missed calls, reminding me that I had silenced his number when I was annoyed with him. Before I got the chance to phone back, my phone lit up with another call.

"Hello? Why is there a damn helicopter landing on my lawn?" I blurted, not giving him the chance to speak.

"Let them in. It's the medical team, and they have Harlem. I couldn't risk him being left alone in the hospital and the person responsible for coming at him again. I didn't get the chance to tell you before, but Harlem said he saw Mya before getting hit. Kymani and I both thought he had to be wrong, but when Ky got there, he saw her too. It's like she doesn't know who either of them is. With all this happening just after all the shit with ya boy Yayo, and at the same time Harlem gets shot, something is going on that we don't know about. It's just too coincidental, and we need to be on the same page so we can figure this shit out."

"I agree. We will be coming back to our issues, but we need to make sure our family is safe first and foremost."

"I'll be back there soon. There is someone we have to pay a little visit to first. Please don't leave the house and keep the kids inside. Security will be pulling up any minute now, but only let Xavier in. The rest will guard the outside, but Xavier is to stay with Harlem at all times."

"Ok. I love you, be careful."

"I love you too, Vee," he expressed before ending the call.

I went about my business, tidying the house and preparing some food to feed everyone. I'm not new to this, and sadly neither are my children. I guess it comes as part of the package. My husband has been in the streets forever, and over the years, any time there is an issue in the streets, he moves all of us up here to the lake and always has us surrounded by security. Lord knows what the neighbors must think.

I stood back and watched as the medical team set up the downstairs bedroom for Harlem, they had machines and devices set up all over the place, and in no time at all, they had set up a whole hospital ward in the downstairs of my house.

Going back into the kitchen, I checked the food in the oven and started preparing the sides. Liberty came downstairs to help me. Even though she is now sixteen, she is very naïve to a lot of things, and that is my fault for trying to shelter her from the life we have.

"Is Harlem going to be ok, ma?" she asked.

"Your brother is a fighter, baby, so I'm sure he will pull through this. He is in God's hands, and we have to trust that he will cover our family in our time of need and protect your brother."

"You are you, daddy, going to get divorced? I know y'all been arguing a lot, and daddy has hardly been home these last few weeks."

"No, we're not going to get a divorce. We're going to work through our problems because that is what you do when you have a problem. You work through it. Both myself and your father have done things we shouldn't have done, and it may take some work, but I'm not prepared to give up on all the years we have together, and neither is he. Everything will be just fine, baby girl, you'll see. Now, help me get this food ready so all of these people your daddy got up in here can eat."

"I love you, mom."

"I love you more, baby."

MY HUSBAND CAME WALKING in the house with Kymani just as the food was being put out. Walking up behind me, he put his arms around my waist and hugged me from behind before whispering in my ear.

"There is something I need to tell you before speaking to everyone else."

I stopped what I was doing and turned to face my husband. Staring at his handsome face, I couldn't help but notice the worried expression he was wearing. There is no denying these last few months have been difficult, but this bullshit is making my husband look old before his time. After all of this is over, I'm taking Harlem on a well-earned vacation. He took my hand and led me outside into the garden, which overlooked the vast lake. We both sat down on the love seat we had installed a few years ago.

"I think one of Yayo's sons is responsible for shooting Harlem. We traced a car caught on the camera back to some little hood rat named Shania that Harlem used to fuck with. She said some little nigga called A.J. was the one who was driving the car. His name is Antonio, which is the name of the eldest boy he had with Ameena. He thinks Harlem killed his mother."

"Even from hell, that motherfucker is causing problems for us. I wish I had told you everything years ago, then you would've killed him, and none of this would be happening now. I'm so sorry."

"That is just the start of it. The girl in the hospital earlier was Heaven. I didn't want to scare her away, and with the way you were acting, it wasn't the time to tell you. I needed to be one hundred percent sure before I got your hopes up, but Havana is Heaven. She went back to the hospital to see Harlem after we had all left, and now, she is missing. At this point, I don't know whether her brother took her, or she was in on the whole thing and set him up."

I almost dropped to the floor hearing my husband speak. The whole time I've been looking for my daughter, she was right there. I was so rude to her, and I hate that her first impression of me was what she saw today.

"We need to find her. I think she looked genuinely

concerned about Harlem at the hospital, so she is a good actress if she is involved. However, if she isn't involved, then she could be in danger. If it were Havana's brother who shot Harlem, then he would've seen her with him. And if he thinks Harlem killed his mom, then maybe seeing his sister with the person he believes is responsible sent him over the edge, and he came back for her. I have failed her for her entire life. I can't fail her again. We have got to find her, please!" I almost pleaded with him.

"We will find her. I promise you. We will bring her back to her family. Havana is as much our child as the others, and I will go to the same lengths as I would for one of them to ensure that she is brought home safely," Big H vowed, pulling me close and kissing my head.

He called everybody into the large dining room so he could tell them all what was happening and what needed to happen next.

"First, I want to thank you all for coming. As you are all aware, my son Harlem was shot this morning after leaving the hospital with his girlfriend, Havana. Kymani has had someone looking at camera footage from around the hospital when the shooting occurred. Luckily, we got to it before the police did, and we have a clear picture of a car leaving the scene. This car is registered to Shania Clark. Some of you will know her as she is an ex-employee and someone Harlem used to fuck with. She had her nose put out of joint when Harlem fired her for bringing too much heat to the organization and starting a fight with his new girlfriend. Shania has admitted that she is responsible for hitting the traps but claims she knew nothing of the shooting. Either way, she signed her own death warrant by fucking with our money, not to mention for the deaths of some of our workers, colleagues, and friends.

The person responsible for hitting the traps, and I suspect the one who pulled the trigger on Harlem, is Antonio or A.J., as he is known. He is believed to be Yayo's eldest son. He has been working alongside his brother and blames Harlem for the death of his mother. Although he has no proof of any involvement at this time, we know that both his mother and Yayo have been missing and are presumed dead, but yet there have been no bodies found," he detailed, knowingly.

"We have Shania in the warehouse and have a couple of heads parked up watching her house in case A.J. returns. Ashlee took Havana back to the hospital before she realized we had flown Harlem out of there, and now Havana is missing. You can believe that the person who was put in charge of her safety is going to pay a heavy price for their fuck up. Now, one thing you should know is that Havana is A.J.'s sister. At this stage, we don't know whether she is involved or has been taken, but until we have proof of anything, we are working on the assumption that she has been taken." Kymani added, standing at the head of the table next to my husband.

"She is my daughter. Yayo told me she had died at birth, but before he was killed, he told me the truth. He has hidden her away from me for all these years, so you see, this vendetta he had against my husband was deeper than a street beef — for him, it was personal. Now we know he is no longer an issue for any of us, but we must remove this next threat before we can move forward. My husband only found out about her a few weeks ago, but none of us knew it is the same girl Harlem has been getting close to," I blurted out.

"Havana is my best friend, and she has been for years, I'm telling you all. She is *not* involved. She would never do something like this, and she would never hurt Harlem. He has done nothing but protect her since the day they met. Even earlier today, she was saying how = Harlem and I are the only people she has left in this world. I am telling you. I know my friend and A.J. must have taken her. She doesn't even like her brothers. They are both idiots, and they don't even really speak to her because her dad always favored her. Plus, they will be pissed when they realize that her dad left everything to her, and they get nothing but a small amount of money," Ashlee added, making me realize that my daughter has been practically under my nose this entire time.

"I want extra workers at all the traps and business locations throughout the entire city. Make sure they stay strapped at all times. I don't care what they are doing. They need to stay ready. If they try to strike again, I want them captured and brought straight to me. I want pictures of A.J., the other brother Alonso, and Havana circulated to every member of this organization and our associates. If any of them take a single fucking step on one of my streets, I want to know about it."

10

HARLEM

One Week Later

I can hear movement around me, but I can't open my eyes. They feel so heavy, almost like I'm asleep, but my brain is awake. My entire body aches, and I can't hear any familiar voices around me. I thought I could hear my dad and Kymani, but unfamiliar people and sounds have replaced those voices. I feel like I'm using all my strength to try to move, just to alert someone to the fact that I'm awake, that I'm here. I don't know where Havana is, but I need to see her face. The last thing I remember is being with her and walking out of the hospital.

Soon, I felt a soft hand holding my own and heard quiet sobs. I knew this was my chance to get help. I tried with all my might to squeeze the hand. Repeatedly, I tried, but I just couldn't do it. At this point, I'm getting pissed off, how my body isn't doing what my brain is telling it to, and there is nothing I can do to make it work. Again, I tried to squeeze with all my strength, but this time I felt something. There was a twitch in my hand, and my eyes fluttered as if they were trying to open.

"His hand, it moved. Please, someone, come and help him. Look, he's trying to open his eyes."

To hear the voice of my little sister made me happy. If she was here, I knew the rest of the family weren't far behind. Before I knew what was happening, I could hear people shuffling around, and then I felt something being pulled from my mouth. I finally opened my eyes to see that my dad and Mama Vee had both come into the room with Ky and Ash behind them.

"Oh, thank you, God!" Ma was crying with her hands together in prayer, she didn't take her eyes off me, and once the doctor stepped back, she ran to me and placed kisses all over my head and face.

"Baby, I'm so happy that you're awake. You had us scared for a while there."

My pops and Ky just walked up beside me and looked at me.

"You scared me, boy," my dad said, bending down and kissing the top of my head. He looks so tired like this has been fucking him up inside.

"Where is Havana?"

"You just need to focus on getting better right now," the doctor advised. "Harlem, this is going to be a long fight. You need to focus on your recovery. I don't want him overdoing it, and we'll need to run some more tests now that he is awake to see the extent of the damage."

"Thanks, Doc," my pops replied while shaking the doctor's hand.

"Where is she? Ma, you don't understand," I stressed. This time I looked at Mama Vee as if I had just remembered that she is Havana's mother.

"It's ok baby. Your daddy told me the truth. Liberty,

please, I need you to get your brother and meet me in the family room. We have to discuss something."

"I overheard y'all talking, and I know that's why you and daddy have been fighting. I know Havana is my sister. I'm not a child so stop treating me like one," Liberty defended, standing up for herself.

"Princess, we will talk about this properly, but you're right. Havana is your sister. I'm sorry for not telling you before, but I only found out she existed a few weeks ago. Your mom was led to believe that she died during her birth and only found out different recently," my dad explained while pulling Liberty under his arm and hugging her close.

"Why the fuck is nobody answering me? Where is Havana?" I asked, getting more irritated by the second. I honestly thought she was a real one, so to find that she isn't here with me hurts like a motherfucker.

"Someone kidnapped her from the hospital, and we don't know where she is. She's been gone a whole week, and we haven't found her," Ashlee blurted out, with tears in her eyes.

"Get me the fuck up! I need to find her!" I ordered, struggling to get my legs to move.

Kymani looked at Ashlee like he wanted to slap the shit out of Ashlee.

"Listen, bro, you not moving. We're on it. We've got everyone and their mama out there looking for Havana. We think her brother has her, so you know he's not gonna hurt her. We'll get her back, bro, and that's on gang," Kymani explained, trying to calm me down.

"Why the fuck would her brother kidnap her?" I asked.

"It's A.J. who is responsible for half the traps getting hit, and he was the one who shot you. He thinks you killed his mama. He's been working with that little *hood rat* bitch

Shania. She denies knowing about the shooting, but she admitted to setting up the traps 'cuz she was pissed with you about firing her ass," my dad added.

"What the fuck is going on? Havana's been gone a whole fucking week, and nobody has found her yet! I want five hundred g's put on this nigga's head. You better tell everyone. I'll pay up the second he is delivered to me dead or alive. I'm not fucking playing. I'm going to kill this motherfucker and send him to hell with his bitch ass mommy and daddy. Get me the fuck up out of here so I can shower. I need a minute to process this shit."

"We did that shit already, bro. The day she got taken, your pops put money on this nigga head but still nobody has found his ass," Ky told me while trying to help me stand.

"Tell them the money just doubled. I want this nigga found. I swear on everything. I'ma make the city bleed behind mine. I want the names and addresses of everyone that motherfucker knows. He has to be somewhere," I demanded, before hobbling toward the bathroom.

I don't care what it takes, I'm going to find my girl, and if one single hair on her head is out of fucking place, I will torture that motherfucker until he begs me to kill him.

My whole body felt like it was on fire the second the water hit my skin. The wounds had already started to heal, but the pain was like nothing I had ever felt before. The feeling of hunger came over me, and I started to feel dizzy from the heat of the shower. I washed off the best I could and got out of the shower. Grabbing a towel, I tied it around my waist and walked back into the room. The second they saw me, they all stopped talking.

"Ma, could you and Lib please get me something to wear? I need to talk to pops and Ky?"

"Of course, I can, baby. Come on, girls, you can make

them all a plate of food while I find him some clothes," ma instructed, making Liberty and Ashlee get up and follow behind her.

"Talk to me," I said.

"I've just had a phone call, and a couple of new addresses have come to light. We've already sent people to check them out, but we're going to have to wait for any news. You look like you gone pass out. Get back in the damn bed. Once we have some food, get them wounds looked at, and you get your pain meds, we can go," my pops advised.

A few minutes later, mama walked in with a pile of clothes and the girls trailing behind her carrying plates of food and bottles of water. Placing them down, they all left the room.

I sat with my pops and Ky while they filled me in on what they had been doing to find Havana. Then the doctor came back in and dressed my wounds before giving me two painkillers. As soon as I swallowed them down with a mouthful of water, I started putting my clothes on, but before I could even make it to my shoes, I felt light-headed. Within seconds, I hit the bed, and my eyes started to close.

"I'm sorry, son, but you need to rest. Trust me, I got this," my dad stated before I drifted into a deep sleep.

11

———

BIG H

I hated to do my son like that, but he was in no fit state to be out in the streets. He needs to give himself time to heal properly. Harlem is physically weak, and he will look weak out there. He has got to trust that we won't let him down. The problem with my son is that he is so used to being alone and unable to depend on anyone that even now, years later, he finds it hard to trust that we will do the right thing by him. I hate that he found out about Vee knowing about Yayo being responsible for shooting Mya 'cuz she is the only person he trusted other than Kymani and me, and now that trust has been broken. I just hope and pray that when I find Havana that she isn't on some flaw shit with my son, because my wife's child or not, I will kill her for playing with my son. Although he is a grown-ass man now, I am still so overprotective of him, and I think a lot of that comes from the fact that I wasn't there for him as a child. Our relationship is strong, and I refuse to let anyone or anything come between us.

I was headed out to meet up with my cousin Richie. We used to be tight back in the day, but our life choices left us on opposite sides. Richie was all for that gang life until he witnessed one of his best friends get taken out in some gang retaliation shit. He was lucky. He survived the shots that were fired into him, and when he woke up, he decided he was out of the gang life. I guess you could say his ass got scared straight. He moved away and went to live with our grandma in New Orleans. He took his ass back to school and climbed the ranks of the NOPD. Recently, he got a transfer back home to care for my auntie and is now the Deputy Chief of Police back here in Chicago. Although our chosen paths kept us from mixing socially, he was family, and we always came through for each other when needed.

WE MET at my auntie's house in Humboldt Park. When I walked in, she was in the kitchen cooking. No matter how old and sick this lady got, she always cooked something. I stopped and spoke with her for a while as it had been a minute since I stopped by to see her. I kissed her on the jaw and handed her some money, before going into the base-ment to find Richie. I promised to come back soon and have a proper visit with Vee and the kids.

"What up, cuz?" he said as he stood to greet me.

We dapped it up before walking over to the bar area he had installed years ago. He poured us both a drink, which I downed in one.

"How's Harlem doing?" he asked, passing me the bottle of Henny.

"He's got my blood running through his veins, so you know he's a fighter. He's awake, but I had the doc sedate him again, or he would be on wilding in the streets. His girl-friend was kidnapped, and I'm certain that the person who shot him has her, and I need help to find out every address linked to this little motherfucker so I can find them both.

"I got you. Just tell me the name, and I'll see what I can find out."

"I appreciate it."

I wrote down the names of the brothers, as well as Yayo and Ameena's names, before handing him the paper.

We sat for a while longer, just shooting the breeze before we said goodbye.

"I'll be in touch soon."

As I left, I stopped to say goodbye to my auntie before heading back to the car.

I pulled onto the I-94 before turning my phone back on. Within seconds the notifications were coming in hard and fast. Looking at the screen, I phoned Ky back as he had sent the most messages.

"Yo, what's good?" I said into the speaker as soon as he answered.

"I've been busy with Tech for the last few hours, but I've finally got a picture of the person who took Havana from the hospital. The dude looks familiar, but I can't place his face. It's not one of her brothers, though. There is another address, a house in Ameena's name. She has only just acquired it, but it's worth a try."

"Send the address over, and I'll meet you there."

"Bet."

I CAME off at the next exit and waited for Kymani to send me the address. I stopped at the gas station to get a drink and some Newports. Within ten minutes, I was back on the road and heading to the address that Kymani had texted to me. I was surprised to see the house was only twenty minutes away from where I was.

When I got outside the house, I noticed a car in the driveway. I sat there for another thirty minutes before noticing Kymani drive past in the opposite direction. Two minutes later, he came jogging back down the block and got into my car.

"Check this out," he said as he held his phone in front of me, showing me a young man's picture.

"Is this who took Havana?"

"Yea, Tech hacked the system again and got that image. He was waiting outside the hospital for her. As soon as he saw her get out of the car with DJ following behind her, he approached DJ. That must've been when he told him that he was one of us."

"Fuck! I know who this fucking kid is."

"Who?"

"It's Harvey. Harlem's little brother," I answered.

I was confused. Why Harvey would be involved?

"He and Harlem were so close until Marlo took him and his sister away. We tried to find them for a long time after he left the city. When we eventually tracked them down, that snitch Marlo threatened to bring down my entire operation, so I knew we had to step back. Harlem had always sworn that when Harvey and Hallie were old enough, he would find them and try to build a relationship with them. This is going to hurt him more than anything."

"What I don't understand is how the fuck is he connected to the brothers. Hold up, look, someone is coming out of the house."

We stopped talking and observed a woman coming out of the house. She went to get something from the car, and as she turned to go back in, I saw her face. Her hair was different, and she looked older, but I would know that face anywhere.

"I swear on everything I love I'm gonna fuck this hoe all the way up!" I barked as I hit the steering wheel.

"Who that?" Ky asked.

"That's Deanna, Harlem's mom."

"Aww, man. This shit just gets even more fucked up by the second. I say we go drag that bitch out of there and shoot anything moving. I bet you this is where they have Havana locked up."

"I think so too, so we must be careful. We need to make sure both of the brothers are in the house when we hit it to get all of them at once."

"Ok, let's get Tye and Tre to come and watch the house. We'll come back when it's dark."

12

———

HARVEY

When I left home a few months ago after an argument with my dad, I came back to Chicago to find my mom. After losing her kids, I thought my mom would've cleaned her act up, but she was even worse when my father took us away from her. All I wanted was to reconnect with my family, but I'm regretting my decision. I should've stayed my ass back in Atlanta with my pops and Hallie.

Within a few days of being back with my mom, I started trying to find my brother. At least if this bitch couldn't help me, then maybe my brother could. Growing up, Harlem was more like a parent to Hallie and me. He was everything to us, which is why it hurt so much that he went with his real dad and forgot all about us. For months after my dad took us, we would pray that Harlem would come back for us, but he never did. It was as if he forgot we even existed.

"Mom, do you have a phone number or an address for Harlem? I need to speak to him. It's not right that he's not helping you," I added since she was always a selfish bitch that I knew I would have to make it all about her. "He should be giving you money and helping to pay bills around this motherfucker. You're his mom at the end of the day. If he knew the state of this place, you know he would help you. Just let me reach out to him."

"Fuck that little nigga! Harlem forgot who the fuck he was the second he left here. As soon as he got a taste of that Big H's money, he never turned his ass around. I have tried to ask him for help, but he flat out refused. I begged him to help me get into a rehab facility to beat this addiction, but he threw a couple of rocks down and told me to go smoke a pipe. He warned me not to come back around him."

"Just let me try. If I spoke to Harlem, I know I could get him to help you," I responded.

"Just let it go, Harvey. He made it clear he done forget where he came from. Do you know that boy drives around the city in a fucking Bugatti? Yea, he got that kind of money, but he can't help his mama. Fuck Harlem and Big H. Both them niggas ruined my life. You know, it was Big H who got me hooked in the first place. He gave me my first pipe and secretly fed my addiction for years. He knew what he was doing. He's a heartless bastard, and now your brother is the same."

Over the next few days, I went out on the streets looking for my brother. I searched for days. I even went over to where I knew Big H had a car wash. My brother used to take me there after school while he worked. I hung around for two days, but the place was never open. I was on my way back to the house when I bumped into Alonso. I knew him from school back in Atlanta. After my pops moved my sister and me away, we went to a school near my grandma's house. That's where I met Alonso. I guess you could say we were friends by default. I hadn't seen him since his dad moved the family back to Chicago but seeing as I didn't know anyone here anymore, I was happy to have someone to chill with. As there were only four black kids in our year group at the uppity ass school we attended, we all formed a friendship. It wasn't long before his brother asked us if we wanted to make some extra money. Of course, I jumped at the chance. Because I had spent all my money making my way to Chicago, I was as broke as a joke and needed a way to make money. I should've known better because as soon as my mom saw me with a little money, she had her hand out, waiting for me to give her some. The first thing she did was go out and score.

The next day when I met up with Alonso and his brother, A.J. told me about a few traps they wanted help to hit. I was down. This time I figured if I could get my mom something to smoke, she would leave my money the fuck alone, but that didn't work. We spent the next week hitting these traps and laying niggas down all over the damn place. It wasn't until after that when I realized that the traps we had hit belonged to Harlem.

One night, I was showering and getting ready to go out when A.J. knocked at the door. He had come to pick me up so he could speak to me without Alonso around. I told him I would be down in ten minutes, so he sat in the living room. When I made it down the stairs, my mom was in the room with him. They were talking, and my mom was flirting. It made me sick how she would constantly throw herself at men, hoping for a little attention. She would do anything, and I mean anything, to get a fix, even if that meant fucking and sucking for some change. It was only at that point that I regretted coming back here.

A.J. was lapping up the attention, and I was shocked to see that he was entertaining the flirting. Before we left, he asked my mom if she wanted to make some money and help him bring down Big H. Of course, she jumped at the chance. She constantly went on about how he ruined her life.

I overheard them talking last night, and this is only the start of their plan. They plan to use the girl to lure Harlem into a trap, so they can kill both him and Big H. Alonso thinks that he'll be able to take over without them around. It's become an obsession with him, and my mother is making it ten times worse by agreeing with everything he says.

When I started all of this, I didn't know that A.J. had orchestrated it all. He had met my mom through his dad, who used to feed her habit to gain information about Big H. She told him I wouldn't be with the plan if I knew it was my brother that we were hitting. Their asses lied to me for weeks, and it was only after I was sent to grab the girl at the hospital that I even knew that she was their fucking sister! They didn't even tell me anything about Harlem being shot until I brought the girl back to the crib. I don't even know if he is ok but hearing A.J. bragging about hitting him five or six times doesn't sound good. It doesn't matter what happened with us. Harlem was still my brother, and I would never knowingly put him in danger. The problem I have is now I'm in over my head, and I don't know how to get out of the fucked-up situation I got myself into.

I feel like such a fucking idiot, but the only way I can think of to redeem myself is to find Big H and explain every-thing. It was a long shot, but I had to try something. I'm just praying that my brother is ok and that this man doesn't kill me before I can make my peace with my brother.

❧

I WENT BACK to the car wash, and this time it was open. I walked in and asked to speak to Big H. The man washing the cars stopped and stared at me.

"Who are you, and what do you want? Bossman is dealing with some family shit right now, so if it's not important, you'll have to come back next week."

"It is important. I have some information on who shot his son." I blurted out.

Before I knew it, two men walked out of the back office. Both of them had their guns drawn and were aiming at me. One of them came and patted me down before leading me back into the office.

"What's your name, kid?" the older of the two men asked me.

"Harvey. I have some information, but I'll only speak to Big H," I relayed, holding my breath.

The way they looked at me, I knew they were ready to fuck me up. The younger of the two men walked up on me as if he would hit me, but the other man told him to sit down.

"Is Harlem ok? I mean, did he survive?" I asked, looking at the older man, but he ignored me and continued scrolling on his phone.

Putting the phone to his ear, he waited.

"I've got some kid at the car wash saying he has some information on who shot Lil' H, but he only wants to talk to you. He said his name is Harvey."

He looked back at me before speaking again.

"Big H said he'll be here in twenty minutes. You can wait in here. He told me that if you try to leave before he gets here, I can shoot you, so sit the fuck down and shut up."

Those twenty minutes seemed like the longest minutes of my life, but when Big H walked in the room, I wanted the ground to open up and swallow me whole.

13

BIG H

"Well, ain't that some shit? It's not every day the motherfucker you're looking for delivers himself straight to the lion's den. You either got some big balls, or you're just plain stupid to turn up like this, kid? Which is it?"

"I'll tell you everything, but please just tell me if my brother is ok?" he almost pleaded.

"He will be. Now speak! You have five minutes to convince me not to kill you today."

"I came back two months ago, hoping to reconnect with my family. I tried to find Harlem, but I couldn't. I even came by here a few times, but y'all were shutdown. On my way back to my mom's crib, I bumped into Alonso. I know him from school back in Atlanta. It was good to have someone here other than my mom. After a little while, his brother A.J. asked me if I wanted to earn some money, so I said yea. He wanted us to hit a few traps. He said they were just some young kids trying to do their thing so there would be no comeback on us. I swear I had no idea they were your and Harlem's traps!

I found out that my mom was in on the whole thing. She set me up to bump into Alonso. She's been working with A.J. this whole time. I didn't find out the truth until after they paid me to grab the girl at the hospital. I didn't even know she was their sister until I got her back to the house that they got us staying in. This whole time I've been back here, my mom has been determined to stop me from reconnecting with my brother. She said you were the one who got her hooked in the first place and secretly fed her habit for years to get your own back on her for some shit she did when y'all were kids. She even went as far as to tell me that she begged Harlem to help her get into rehab, but he just threw some rocks at her and told her to get the fuck on. I know now that they've all been playing me. I knew nothing about Harlem getting shot until the girl was begging them to tell her if he was ok.

I swear, I never would've got involved if I'd known it was you and Harlem they were after. A.J. has got some mad hate for you. He said you took everything off his dad and that all your empire should've been his."

"Let's just clear a few things up. I never gave your mom crack in my life and both your brother and I have tried numerous times to get her into a rehab facility. Every time your brother sees her, he asks her again to get clean for y'all kids. I found the house earlier today, and I saw Deanna, so what you're telling me doesn't shock me. When I got the footage of you leaving the hospital with Havana, I wanted to kill you. Are you prepared to help me get Havana out of there and kill the rest of them? Harlem will make the decision about what to do with Deanna, but she is a snake and always has been. Ever since the first line of cocaine touched that woman's nostril, she changed into someone I didn't recognize but to stoop as low as do to this to her child is a different level of fucked up."

"I'll do whatever you want me to."

"Why did you come back here, and where is Hallie?"

"I came back to reconnect with my brother and ask for his help. Hallie is mixed up in some shit in Atlanta, and I needed his help," Harvey relayed, making me want to know more.

"What kind of shit? And where is that fuck nigga daddy of yours?"

"Man, that motherfucker has been gone for the last three years. He met some woman and left us at the crib with my grandma. We ain't heard nothing from him. He just pays the bills and sends money to grandma for groceries and shit.

After fighting with grandma about her boyfriend, Hallie has been gone almost six months now. This nigga named Keys, and he's all about that gang life, but he's still trying to earn his stripes. He'll do anything for clout, and she's in danger. He's always getting her into some shit, and he treats her like crap. She's so stupid and in love. She thinks they're some modern-day Bonnie and Clyde. I heard about him jacking a shipment that belonged to someone much higher up in another gang, and they want to kill him and anything close to him, including Hallie. I've begged her to leave, but she doesn't listen to me. She still treats me like I'm a fucking kid just because she is eighteen months older than me. I hoped Harlem would be able to talk some sense into him."

"We tried to find you after he took you from your moms that day. He warned us that if either of us came near you, he would bring down my entire operation. Harlem has been waiting for the day you were old enough to be able to reach out to you. He'll be happy to see you, and you've got the chance to redeem yourself by bringing Havana home," I told him.

Kymani walked into the office just as I finished speaking.

"The whole crew is ready to fuck some shit up," he said, staring at Harvey. "You lucky you my nigga's brother, or I'd shoot your ass little boy."

After hearing everything that Harvey had to say, I decided he was telling the truth. The boy was clearly scared, and more than anything, Harlem would be pissed that he's been here looking for him while Hallie was out there in trouble. I just hope it's not too late to help her, or he will never forgive himself. Harlem was more than a brother to them kids. He was both of their parents rolled into one. He had to do everything for them, and they were good kids.

"Harvey, I need you to go back to the house and act like everything is normal. I want you to text me and tell me when both brothers and your mom are all there. As soon as I give you the word, you get Havana and get out. I'll have a car waiting behind the house to take you and Havana away from there while we go in and deal with the rest of them."

"Ok. Thank you for believing me. I swear, I won't let you down."

"Ky, can you drop Harvey back at the house? I need to go and check on a few things."

14

HAVANA

It feels like I've been locked in this fucking room forever. I swear on everything I love I'ma kill my fucking brothers. Knowing that my brother killed Harlem is tearing me apart. I'm going out of my mind. I don't care that they are the only family I have left. I will make sure they both pay for this with their lives. I just hope that Harlem's family doesn't blame me for what A.J. and Alonso have done. I don't know who the fuck the woman with A.J. is, but she knows both Harlem and his dad, judging by the sounds of it. Between her and my brother, you would think Harlem had done something horrible to them, but I just don't see it. The shit that they are saying doesn't match the man I know and have come to love.

They only bring me out of the room twice a day to eat meals with them, but I would rather they just leave me the fuck alone. The only thing I have in the room with me is the TV they never turn on and a pile of old books. A.J. keeps saying that he is sending me back to Atlanta, but he hasn't even left the house in days, so I don't know how the fuck he thinks he can get me all the way to Atlanta. I think they know they've fucked up. They are all agitated and jumpy as fuck. I hope this means they're going to make a mistake and that I will be able to get free before I lose my damn mind.

The sound of the bedroom door opening made me jump. I turned and saw the same guy who took me from the hospital coming into the room. Since I have been here, he has been the only one who has tried to be friendly, which I think is a joke, considering it's his ass who kidnapped me.

"I have to be quick, A.J. and my mom is asleep, and Alonso is outside on the phone. I've found a way to get us out of this. Just be ready to go tonight. This is all going to be over soon." He handed me a soda and a bag of chips, but before I got the chance to ask anything else, he quietly closed the door, locking it as he left.

I don't know how he thinks we will get out of here, but if there is a chance I can get away from here, I'm taking it. I just have to hope that his plan works.

I settled back into the book I'd been reading and lost myself in a world that I could only dream of. If there is one thing I know after all of this, it's that I need to make sure I always have my gun with me and learning to shoot correctly is a must. Just think, if I'd have finished Tip off the first time I shot him, then he wouldn't have been able to come back at me, and I wouldn't have ended up in the hospital, and Harlem might still be here with us.

So much time had passed that it was dark outside, and I was losing hope that the young boy's plan would work. Suddenly, there was a loud noise from downstairs, and a few seconds later, the door to the room came bursting open.

"Quick, we have to go now. You have to just trust me,

please," the same guy relayed as he grabbed my hand and dragged me down the corridor. We made our way into another one of the bedrooms, and he locked the door behind him.

"Listen, we will have to lower ourselves down on the porch, then climb down the side. Do you think you can manage that? We have to do this now."

"Ok. Let's do it," I replied.

He went first and then helped me onto the porch. Turning around, he lowered himself down as far as possible before letting go and landing on his feet. I followed suit and did the same. As we ran away from the house, I could hear what sounded like gunshots and glass breaking. I didn't even stop and turn around. I followed behind my savior until we got to a waiting car. As soon as we opened the door to get in, I instantly recognized the driver as one of Big H's men. He was at the hospital guarding Harlem when I left.

"Are you ok, sweetheart? Did they hurt you?"

"I'm just happy to be out of there."

"So, kid, you really Harlem's little brother?"

"Yes, sir," he said with his dead down in shame.

"You're his brother?" I asked, not masking the shock in my voice.

"I'm sorry. I needed money, and A.J. asked me if I was down to hit a few traps, so I said yes. I never knew they were anything to do with my brother. I didn't know Harlem had been shot, and I didn't know that you were their sister. They told me you stole from them and that I had to get you so they could get whatever it was that you took, and they would let you go. I'm so fucked up! I swear I should've just stayed my ass in Atlanta. I just needed to find my brother, and now I've fucked it all up. He's going to hate me for this."

"Kid, I know how many times that boy has tried to find

you over the years. I remember how close y'all used to be. Your dad had no right to take you the way he did. You never should've been cut off from Harlem. He was everything to you and Hallie growing up. I know your brother will forgive you, not to mention you just saved his woman. It'll be alright, mark my words."

"He's alive?" I asked.

"Yes, Harlem's awake now. It's going to take a minute to heal up properly, but he's going to be fine. I can't say the same for your brothers or his mom, though."

"D is his mom? What the fuck kind of shit is that? She's as bad as my mom and dad. Our parents are all fucked up!"

"Crack does fuck up things to people. It's not either of your faults that your parents are so fucked up. I'll be honest with you, Deanna has been on a downward slope since she was seventeen, but she's got worse in the last few years. We've tried to get her into rehab hundreds of times, but that woman is not interested in trying to change her life. As for Yayo, he's been fucked in the head for as long as I can remember. You know him and Big H used to be close as hell, but he got too big for his boots, and when he got arrested, he decided to snitch on everyone. Many of us did time behind him, running his mouth the way he did. Y'all are not your parents. You can choose the life you want to live. Take it from an old man who knows."

15
____

HARLEM

When I woke up from whatever the fuck it was that doctor gave me, I was heated as hell. How the fuck did my pops just get me drugged? Where the fuck do they do that shit at, man? I looked out of the window, and it was dark outside, so I knew whatever he had the doctor give me knocked my ass clean out for hours.

I went to stand, but Xavier ran to my side and helped me up.

"You need to take it easy, Lil' H."

"I need to find Havana."

"Trust your pops. He's got this under control. Havana is safe. Come on, let's get you something to eat."

We walked into the kitchen and saw my mom sitting at the island drinking a glass of wine. She looked like she had been crying, but as soon as she noticed us, she wiped her face and stood up.

"Baby, I'm so happy to see you up and moving around. Let me get you some food."

"I need a phone. I need to call pops," I said, just as I heard the front door opening.

"I can't believe you drugged me. You ain't serious!" I argued as he rounded the corner and entered the room, with Kymani following behind him.

"Serious as fucking heart attack! What the fuck I look like letting you go do shit like that when you still got holes all over you? Those wounds haven't even healed yet! Boy, you thought you were going to fuck shit up not even an hour after your eyes opened, not on my watch. Now sit the fuck down and chill for a minute!"

"How do you expect me to chill when Havana is missing? She could be hurt, or even worse, dead! I'll chill when I find my girl!" I rubbed my hands down my face in frustration.

"She's fine. She's on the way here now with your Uncle Rock. But before she gets here, I need to tell you something, and you're not going to like it. Let's go out back and smoke while we talk."

I followed my dad outside and sat on one of the loungers that Liberty and Ashlee had just vacated.

"Is she hurt?" I asked.

"No, son, she's not hurt. Her brothers had her. They think you killed their mom, and Yayo filled their heads with shit about me, so they wanted to take us out and stage a takeover."

"How do we know she wasn't in on the plan?"

"I almost wish she were because it would be an easier pill to swallow. I know who they were working with, and I wish I didn't have to tell you this. I'm sorry, son, but Deanna was working with them, and they roped Harvey in on the plan too. He came to see me at the car wash, and he was scared. He knew the brothers from Atlanta but bumped into them when he was out trying to find you. He's been here a few weeks, but we had everything shut down because of Yayo. When the opportunity came for him to hit a few traps with them, he jumped at the chance, but he swears he didn't know they were ours, but he needed the money. You know I am a good judge of character, and I believe him. Harvey got Havana out of there while we went and dealt with the rest of them. I told him that when I message him, he had to get her and climb out the window and down the porch. Your Uncle Rock was waiting behind the house in the car. He took them to get some food, but they're on the way here now."

"Where is Deanna now?"

"She's in the warehouse with the brothers right now. I've got Tre and Enzo watching them. It took all my strength not to shoot the bitch on sight, but I can't be responsible for what happens to her next. Only you can make that call. She's still your mom, so if you want to try to help her again, I'll stand by your decision, but the brothers have both got to go."

"I don't even know what to say at this point, but she's never going to change. I need to think about that. I don't know if I can be responsible for ending my mom's life. What is Harvey doing here? And where is Hallie?"

"Harvey came to find you because Hallie is in trouble. I'll let him tell you the rest when he gets here."

As we stood to go back inside, my pops grabbed me and pulled me into a hug.

"No matter what happens on this earth, I got you. You're never going to be alone. I'm always going to be right by your side. Don't let this shit with your mom get inside your head. We will deal with shit accordingly and come out stronger than ever. Everything will work out fine just trust me. I love you, son."

"I love you too, pops. You and Kymani are the only people I trust. I know you always got my back, and I'm thankful for you. You took me out of a fucked-up situation and gave me a life I never thought possible. Mama Vee is the only mom I need, but that doesn't mean I'm forgiving her right now. She never should've hidden the fact that Yayo killed Mya. I could've got at his old ass a long time ago. Shit! Mya! Pops..."

"I know, I saw her too. That's another problem for another day, though. We'll get to the bottom of that shit, too. It looks like it will be a long hot summer in Chicago. Don't let your past fuck up your future. By that, I mean, don't let the fact that Mya is alive get in the way of your relationship with Havana."

"I know, I know. It's just fucked up. Mya looked straight through me like she didn't even know who the fuck I was. On everything, I'ma kill her fucking parents for this shit. I went through years of hurt after losing her the way I did, but she was alive and being hidden from me the whole time. That's some fuckery right there."

We went back inside the house just as my uncle's car pulled up in the driveway. Seconds later, Uncle Rock walked in, followed by Harvey and Havana. The second she saw me she ran into my arms. I just held her tight and let her cry on my chest.

"I thought you were dead."

"Na baby, it takes more than that to kill a real thug," I said, kissing the top of her head.

"I'm going to kill them. A.J. and Alonso, they did this."

"I know, baby, my pops just told me. Did they hurt you?" I asked, still holding onto her.

"Alonso hit me a few times, but it's nothing," she admitted shyly, realizing that the whole family was standing there watching us. I straightened up but kept one arm around Havana.

I turned and looked at my little brother. He looked like he was scared for his life.

"Don't just stand there, bro, come here," I said, pulling him into a hug.

"I'm sorry," was all he said.

"We got time to talk about all that. I got you, though. Lib, could you show Harvey up to the guest room on the second floor, so he can get cleaned up and get him some clothes of mine to put on," I instructed, watching my brother and sister walk away.

I turned to look at Mama Vee. She was standing there with a tear-streaked face.

"Baby, this is Mama Vee. Ma, this is Havana."

They both just stared at each other for a second, and for the first time, I could see how much they looked alike. They both hugged each other and cried.

"I'm so sorry," ma said as he held onto Havana.

"I know the truth. My dad told me he lied to you. I don't blame you, but this is a lot for me to get my head around. I just need some time to process everything that's been happening, and then I hope we can get to know each other properly," Havana stated, pulling back and nestling back under my arm.

"I'll show you to our room and have Ashlee bring you some clothes."

"Ashlee has my bag. I left it in the car when I got out at the hospital," Havana noted, following behind me.

When we got into the room, I left her to shower and went to find Ashlee. I walked down the corridor to Ky's room and knocked on the door. Hearing Ashlee shout out that it was ok to enter, I walked inside.

"Ash, Havana said you've got her bag in the car."

"Yea, I'll get it now. Is she in your room?"

"Yea, she's in there. She's in the shower, but that's your best friend, so she won't mind. I'm gonna smoke something with Ky, and then I'll be back in there."

I turned to Ky the second Ashlee walked out of the door.

"What do you make of what Harvey is saying? You think he straight?"

"I'ma always keep it one hundred with you, bro. At first, I was skeptical. He just turned up one day after all that shit went down, but after speaking to him, I think he's being straight with us. I had Tech look into it. He checked the school records, and Harvey and Alonso were both in the same school at the same time. His story checks out about the car wash being closed. Harvey was desperate, and they took advantage of him. It's Deanna that's the problem. She knew exactly what she was doing, and from what Harvey says, she knew about the plan to shoot you. She's too far gone bro, and I don't think you can help her. You know what has to be done," Ky relayed, passing me the blunt.

As I sat smoking the blunt, I thought about everything that had happened over these last few months. I know in my heart that what Ky is saying is right, but I don't know if I can be responsible for killing the woman who gave me life.

"I know, bro, but..." I just shook my head.

"You need to take a minute and process shit. Go and chill with Havana. We'll deal with anything else tomorrow. I know my ass needs to sleep. I don't think I've slept beside Ashlee for weeks. Your pops and I have been hitting the streets hard. I'm happy you're awake, though. After the number of hits you took, you had me worried for a minute."

Looking at my bro, Kymani looked like the weight of the world was on his shoulders. I can imagine how hard he was going to find the person responsible 'cuz I would've been the same if it was him in my position.

"Five shots couldn't drop me. I took it and smiled. Now I'm back to set the record straight. With my AK, I'm still the thug that they love to hate... I'll hit em' up," I said, rapping the lyrics to Tupac's "Hit 'Em Up".

"Nigga, you got hit six times. Shut the fuck up with your old ass lyrics. You sound like your pops," Ky joked, laughing at me.

"Man, you always trying to fuck up my vibe," I replied, sharing the laugh with my boy. "I appreciate you though, for real. We gonna take a vacation when the dust settles. I don't know about you, but a nigga could do with a break."

"For real. It's good to have you back, bro," he replied. We dapped it up, and I headed back to my room.

16

HAVANA

Iburst into tears the second Harlem left me alone in the room. I then went into the bathroom and stripped out of my clothes. I turned the water on, climbed into the shower, and sat on the floor crying. I've spent the last week thinking Harlem was dead, so to finally see with my own eyes that he is ok brought a wave of emotion over me. However, my mind quickly snapped back to my brothers. Now that I know Harlem is safe, it's as if all the feelings that I have been suppressing just bubbled over and exploded like a volcano erupting.

I know I'd never been close to A.J. and Alonso, but to think they wanted to hurt me the way they did still has me feeling some type of way. And I really can't get over the fact that Harlem's mom was involved and not only condoned what A.J. was doing but encouraged it. We really do have some fucked up parents.

I hope Vee didn't think I was being rude earlier, but I need time to get my thoughts straight. In the space of three months, my entire world, as I knew it, has been ripped from under me, and I haven't even had time to catch my breath before more shit is thrown at me.

I heard a knocking at the bathroom door. Thinking it was Harlem I stood up and turned so he couldn't see my face.

"It's only me. I just came to check on you," I heard Ashlee say as she walked into the bathroom.

I finished washing my body and my hair before stepping out of the shower and wrapping my towel around me.

"I'm not ok. Ash, my whole life is fucked up. Everything I knew is gone, over, finished. I don't know what I am going to do. I'm paranoid that something else will happen, and I don't know how much more I can handle."

"You're going to get through it. Your old life might be over, but your new life is just starting. Plus, not everything is gone. I'm still here. I'm not going anywhere. We're in this for life, bitch," she noted, pulling me into an embrace. "You need to get some sleep. You can relax now. You're safe. Harlem is awake, and there are at least ten men outside with huge ass rifles. Nothing bad is going to happen."

"I ain't ever gonna let anything happen to you again, baby girl," Harlem chimed in from the doorway.

"You two are all I've got," I mumbled.

Ashlee hugged me again before telling us she was going back to bed, leaving Harlem and me alone.

I searched inside my bag for some clothes to wear while Harlem got in the shower. When he came back into the room wearing nothing but his towel, I couldn't help noticing the wounds on his body that hadn't yet properly healed, but he still looked so fine to me. He awakened something inside me, and I needed to be with him. After the whirlwind of these last few months, we haven't even had the chance to have sex yet, and right now, that is all I can think about.

The whole time my brothers had me locked up in that room, thinking Harlem was dead broke my heart, but now that I know he is ok, I have this overwhelming need to keep him close to me.

As if he could read my mind, he came up behind me and slid his arms around my waist. Placing soft kisses on my neck, I could feel my knees weaken from his touch.

"I missed you," he admitted into my ear before turning my body around to face him.

"I missed you too. I thought you were dead. This whole time they led me to believe that you were gone. I'm so happy to be here with you," I stressed, reaching up and kissing Harlem passionately while tears ran down my face.

Harlem picked me up and wrapped my legs around his waist. The towel he was wearing fell, and I could feel his rock-hard dick stroke me as he held me.

"You're going to hurt yourself. Lay down, baby. We've got forever. All of that can wait until your body is healed," I stated, noticing the pained look on his face. "Let me look after you for a change." I lowered my feet to the ground and eased his naked body back to the bed.

I got the things I needed to wash and change his bandages. I took my time to ensure each wound was clean before applying the clean bandage. I made my way down his body, kissing where each scar was forming. Stopping when I got to Harlem's throbbing erection, just the thought of his dick was making me wet.

Reaching out, I took it in my hand. Placing soft kisses over the head, I felt it harden from my touch. Looking up at Harlem, I took his length into my mouth, closed my lips around him, and started sucking. I stared into his eyes the entire time I worked his massive dick in and out of my mouth, keeping my teeth from touching him. I've only ever given head a couple of times, so hopefully, I'm doing it to his liking. Tip used to roughly pull my head up and down until I was choking, but Harlem was so gentle. He keeps stroking my face, soft moans escaping his lips. Never in my life have I wanted to please someone as much I do this man.

Standing up, I pulled my shorts down straddled him again, easing my soaking wet pussy onto his dick. I started rocking back and forth slowly before bouncing my ass up and down.

"I've been waiting to feel that pussy since the day I met you, and it's as good as I knew it would be. Keep going, baby, just like that," he urged softly.

"Mmmm, this dick feels so good, Harlem," I expressed, getting into the rhythm and riding him as if my life depended on it. Within minutes, we were both cumming, and I fell onto his chest and tried to catch my breath.

Sleep found me easily after that. Finally, my mind could rest, if only for a minute. All that matters is that Harlem is ok, and we are finally together. My mind drifted to Dr. Grayson. I don't know what the deal is with her and Harlem, but I plan on finding out. I refused to allow her to come along and fuck up my happily ever after.

17

———

A.J

I knew I was risking a lot by trusting a crackhead, but I was quickly running out of options. Shania's ass has been MIA for a minute, and I had to assume that Big H got her already. I'm not bothered, she had her uses, but I got everything I needed out of her. I would've kept her around for that fire ass head she be giving, but I don't care enough to look for her.

I thought Deanna would be my problem, but as long as I kept her high, she did whatever the fuck I told her to do. On the other hand, this little nigga Harvey was proving to be a pain in my ass. I had to keep him around because that was the deal I made with Deanna, and I might have to use her to pull Harlem out of hiding if my plan failed.

Over the last few days, I've been watching him, and ever since he found out about Harlem getting shot, he has been acting differently. When he went out earlier, I had him followed right to Bug H's car wash. I thought I had time to put a plan into action, but when my guy told me he was in a car on his way back here with one of Harlem's boys, I knew I had to move fast. I grabbed all my money and guns and got the fuck out of dodge.

Yea, I know, I'm flaw as fuck for not at least taking my brother with me, but it's every man for himself at this point. Alonzo knew the risks when he got involved in this shit. I had a feeling something like this would happen, which is why I got my cousin Zain from Atlanta to come and stay at the crib. That nigga looks just like me, and anyone that didn't know us could easily mistake us for one another. By the time they realize that he's not me, I'll be long gone.

I'd been driving for around two hours when I decided to check into a hotel and order some food. While I was waiting for my order, I opened up the app on my phone for the cameras in the house. It looked like everything was normal for a while, but then I saw Harvey and Havana climbing out of the window just as the house was stormed with men carrying AKs. I watched Alonso, my cousin, and Deanna all get dragged out of the house. The camera which overlooked the driveway showed them being bundled into the back of a black van.

Fuck!!

My whole fucking plan has just gone out of the window. I don't know what I'm going to do now, but I know I need I lie low and figure some shit out. First thing tomorrow, I'm taking my ass back to Atlanta until I build a stronger crew. I'll come back stronger than ever, and one thing is for certain, this isn't the last that motherfucking Harlem has seen of me. As for my snake ass sister, she's on my hit list too. She picked her sides when she started fucking the enemy. They don't realize it yet, but the worst person to have as an enemy is someone with nothing left to lose.

18

HARLEM

Laying here with Havana in my arms is the happiest I've felt in a long time. I could stay like this forever, but I know we still have some work to put in before I can completely relax. Once I was sure Havana was asleep, I went to find my brother. It's time I sat Harvey down and find out what the fuck has been going on and where the hell Hallie is.

Knocking on his door, I opened it to find him sitting on the bed watching a film.

"Yo, I thought I'd come and check on you. Did you have some food?"

"Yea, thanks. Liberty brought some up to me. I felt awkward sitting down there with everyone watching me like I'm the enemy. I swear I didn't know they would shoot you, and I didn't know they were your traps. I swear, I would never do anything to hurt you."

"You have to know that you are the enemy to them. You're only alive off the strength that you're my brother. It is imperative that you tell me the whole truth about every-thing 'cuz things still ain't adding up for me. You can start by telling me how the fuck you ended up working with A.J. and Alonso and why the hell Deanna is involved."

I rolled a blunt and sat out on the balcony, listening while my brother told his story. From the time he landed in Chicago to the time he turned up at the car wash, Harvey told me everything he had done and every person he'd spoken to. With everything that has transpired over the last few months, I knew I had to process what he was telling me. My trust has been shattered recently, so at this point, I only trust what I can see until proven otherwise.

"Listen, you need to understand that a lot of shit has been happening these last few months, and my trust is at an all-time low. I'm still getting over that fuck nigga A.J. shooting me and my girl getting kidnapped, so you have to give me a bit of time. Also, I know that I still have to decide what I'm going to do with Deanna. By all rights, she signed her own death warrant for fucking with me and my pops the way she has. But using my brother to try to bring me down is a new low, even by her standards. The only reason she is still breathing is that she birthed me. From this point forward, you're either with me or against me."

"I'm with you. I'll prove myself to you and earn back your trust."

"I'm tired, and I need to lay up under my girl. Tell me about Hallie before I go."

"Man, Hallie is all kinds of fucked up. Our dad walked out a few years ago, and we haven't seen his ass since. We have been living with my grandma, and he just sends money and shit but never comes around. About a year ago, Hallie got involved with this nigga named Keys. Ever since then, she has been banging with him and his crew. Around six months ago, she had a huge fight with grandma, and she hasn't been home since. Recently they robbed the wrong nigga, and word on the street is that when he finds Keys, he will kill him and anyone close to him. Every time I try to see her, she makes excuses because she won't come. And the one time she did come, he didn't leave me alone with her for a single second. He's controlling, and he treats her like shit, but she thinks they on their Bonnie and Clyde shit."

"Let me talk to my pops and see the best way to handle this shit. I need more information on this little nigga and the motherfucker looking to kill them. We'll talk about this more in the morning. Try to get some sleep.

With that, I left Harvey and made my way back to my bedroom. I couldn't wait to get back in my bed and just be with Havana.

I'm not thinking about any of this shit until tomorrow, and once I deal with all this shit, I'm taking Havana away on vacation.

19
____

BIG H

Since I made the choice to get out of the game, it feels as if I'm being dragged back in more and more each day. I promised Vee that I would hand the reigns over to Harlem and concentrate on my family and my legit businesses. Still, with everything going on these last six months, it's been impossible. I'm tired of this life now. I want to be able to relax and enjoy the fruits of my labor, but nothing is ever that simple.

It was never my plan to still be in the game when I was hitting forty, but here the fuck I am. After I help Harlem sort out this problem with his sister, I'm retiring. Since I came out of the pen, I've been putting things into place so that I can hand everything over to my son. My team already knows the deal. It's time for us to step back and let the younger generation do their thing. We've made enough money that we could've turned our back on this shit a long time ago. None of us need to be out running the streets anymore. We've just been doing that shit for fun.

My brother Rock and I have just signed the paperwork for our next venture. We're now co-owners of a private members club. It's in a quiet spot, half an hour from the city. It's somewhere for my crew to hang out now that we're retiring. There will be a fully stocked bar and some games tables. We're even installing a few poles and a stage. Shit, we are retiring, not dying. a nigga still needs to see some ass and titties.

I know I need to sit down and talk to my wife. Divorce is not an option, and I'm sure as fuck not ready to throw away our marriage. We need to fix this shit, and it's going to take time, but we have to get back to our happy place. I can't bear thinking of life without my wife, and these last few weeks have been hell on me. I know I fucked up and took things too far with Imani's crazy ass, and that's before I even knew about Heaven, so I've got no excuse. I have never stepped out on my wife in all my years of marriage, and I wish I never did it. I was locked up, angry with my wife, and horny. At first, it was just harmless flirting, but then she made it clear she wanted me. She would come in wearing the tightest little skirts, with those long sexy legs that she would cross and uncross constantly, flashing her freshly waxed pussy. It got too much to handle, so I did what any man in my situation did. I let her suck my dick. I'm not even going to the front. The fact that there were guards right outside and we could get caught made it even more exciting. It got to where she would come by daily just to get some dick. I would be fucking her senseless with my hand over her mouth to stop her from screaming out, but it was the hottest sex of my life.

I've seen her a few times since I got out, and I know I'm wrong, but I needed a nut. You know what they say, better the devil, you know. At least I didn't go out looking for new pussy. The problem is now she's hooked on the dick and is threatening to tell my wife if I don't keep seeing her. Yea, I bet you're laughing now. *Silly motherfucker should've known.* I need to deal with this shit first because I'm gonna have to beg like Keith Sweat to get my wife to forgive me, and I can't have anything getting in the way.

I grabbed my coffee and sat down in my recliner, which I'd situated right next to the French window in my office to look out over the vast lake. I watched in awe at the beautiful colors lighting up the sky as the sun rose. This is my favorite part of the house, mainly because it's the only room I can smoke in without Vee nagging but also because it has the most breathtaking view over the lake. When we're here, I spend hours sitting here watching the world. This is my thinking spot.

I lit the blunt I'd left in the ashtray last night and sat back. Taking a deep breath and inhaling the weed, I held it for a few seconds before exhaling my troubles along with the smoke. I don't know how today will go, and I don't know if my son will ever be the same again if he has to kill his own mom. This will be a test to see if Harlem is ready to be in charge. Sometimes, as the boss, you have to make hard decisions, but a snake will always be a snake. Deanna has overstepped the mark this time, and regardless of Harlem's choice today, she is a dead woman. If he decides she can walk away from this, I'm certain that she will soon have an overdose and die.

I could hear footsteps in the kitchen, so I went to see who else was up at this time of day. I was surprised to see Harlem and Kymani sitting at the breakfast bar eating cereal. The sight reminded me of when they were in school. I was always coming home to find them sitting around eating all my damn cereal and drinking up all my milk.

"I didn't think either of you would be up this early."

"I want to go to the warehouse and get this over with. I've

been thinking about it all night, and she'll never change. If I let my mom walk away from this, there will always be a chance that she will try to come at us again."

"You're doing the right thing, son. Have you spoken to Havana about her brothers yet?" I replied.

"Not yet. I don't know what she's going to say. This is a lot for her," he answered,

I turned to see Havana walking down the stairs.

"I'm not stupid. I was born into this life, so I know what it is. Snakes don't make it out here without getting killed. It's them or us, and I'm choosing us every time," she noted, looking lovingly at Harlem and going to stand in front of him.

"Me too, baby. It's always us over them," he agreed, kissing her softly.

"I'm coming with you, though. I want to show them I'm not scared of them, plus I owe them motherfuckers some payback. They have to go to hell knowing that I chose you."

"Ok, killa. Get that ass back upstairs and get ready," Harlem advised, slapping Havana's ass as she turned around.

"We'll be ready to go in half-hour. Actually, make that an hour," Harlem said with a laugh as he followed her out of the room.

"Nasty ass motherfucker! All you are thinking about is your dick, and we got shit to do," Kymani fussed, but Harlem was gone.

"You might as well come into my office and smoke something while we wait for them," I suggested, hitting Ky on the shoulder.

"He's lucky I don't just go and shoot all of them motherfuckers myself and leave him to clean up the mess."

20

HAVANA

When I saw that Harlem had followed me back up to our room, I assumed he wanted to talk about what I had just said, but he had other ideas. He grabbed me, pulling me close before kissing me passionately. Lifting my top over my head, he softly kissed my neck before making his way down further and sucking on my nipples. He pulled my shorts down with ease and inserted two fingers inside my already soaking wet box. I couldn't help but moan as Harlem worked his fingers in and out of me while biting my nipples gently.

"You're so fucking sexy, ma. The way you bossed up has got me rocked up," he admitted, looking straight into my eyes with a smile before pulling his fingers out and licking them with passion written all over his face.

Harlem pushed me back on the bed and lifted my legs. Before I even knew what was happening, he started licking and sucking on my clit. As much as I was trying to be quiet, I couldn't stop the screams from escaping my lips. I ground my hips into his hot mouth and rode the waves of the orgasm he was delivering. My legs and pussy were still shaking as he stood up and put his dick inside me. Unlike last night, when he made love to me, this was more intense fucking. Harlem stared into my eyes as he thrust in and out of me with urgency. Within minutes, he had me shaking and screaming into another mind-blowing orgasm as we both came at the same time. He collapsed onto the bed and pulled me on top without even taking his dick out of me. Slowly, I rocked back and forth while kissing him passionately.

"You're my everything, Harlem. I've never felt anything like this before. I love you so much," I professed as I increased the pace.

"I love you too, Havana. It's me and you against the world, ma."

Sex with Harlem is like nothing that I've ever experienced before. I had to close my eyes to stop the tears that were forming. This man was going to be my forever. I could feel it.

After another round, we both headed into the shower. We got ready quickly and made our way back downstairs.

THE DRIVE over to the warehouse was quiet. I sat in the back of the car with Harlem while Ky was upfront with Big H driving. Everyone seemed to be lost in their thoughts, but a few minutes before we pulled up, Kymani turned and looked at me.

"Are you sure you're ready to do this, Vana? There's no going back after you walk in there, and I don't want you to do anything you'll regret later. You don't have to do this. Even a real thug would find it hard to pull a trigger on their own family. You can just let us handle this for you. You don't need to get your hands dirty."

"I'm ready. I'm so sick of people walking all over me. They've always been assholes, but if my daddy were here, he would never let them get away with what they've done. I have to do this," I stressed, hearing my voice break as I spoke the words.

"He's right, baby, you don't gotta do this. We got you."

21

HARLEM

Pulling up at the warehouse with my pops, Ky, and Havana, I finally felt ready to do what I knew needed to be done. I had to kill my mom. In a way, I'm sad that it came to this, but she made her choices, so it's fuck her. I don't know how she can live with herself. She used one son to try to fuck up the other but sending a nigga to shoot her oldest child is a fucking joke. That shit sealed the deal as far as her life is concerned. I would've had sympathy for her, being as though she has a monkey on her back, but she's had too many chances with me.

Havana tightened her grip around my hand when we walked in as she looked from one person to the other. I could see that my boys had done a number on these motherfuckers, and I was happy to see that they didn't go easy on them. These motherfuckers almost cost me my life, so it's only right they pay with theirs.

"So, you motherfuckers thought you would get away with what you did to my girl and me, and there would be no repercussions?" I asked as I stood in front of them.

"Harlem, baby, you don't have to do this. They tricked

me into helping them. Just help mama get clean, please. We can work on our relationship. I promise I'll be the mom y'all deserve."

"It's too late for that, Deanna. You set me up to get hurt and used my brother to rob me. All you had to do was get clean, and I would've forgiven you for everything. I tried to help you several times, but that glass dick you love so much be more important than your fucking kids!" I spat before turning to the brothers. "As for you little niggas, you fucked up when you came at me and got caught."

Havana launched herself forward and started hitting her brother. Alonzo just looked at her and smiled, spitting out the blood that formed in his mouth from the punches she delivered.

"Do your worst, you little bitch. Daddy ain't here to protect you now. Watch what happens to you."

"You can't do shit to me, nigga! You don't honestly think you're getting out of this, do you?"

"You wouldn't let them kill your brother. You don't have the heart to do. Stop playing and tell them to let me go."

"I'm my daddy's daughter, motherfucker. I'll show you how much heart I have," Havana defended, pulling a pink gun out of the back of her pants and shooting him in the knee. "You thought you could put hands on me, and I would have mercy on you? Fuck you! You can rot in hell with your whore of a mother."

She turned to the other brother, who was still knocked out and kicked him. He lifted his head and looked at her.

"Zain?" she asked, confused. "This isn't A.J. This is my cousin, Zain. That means A.J. is out there still."

"Where the fuck is A.J.?" I said, grabbing him by the hair, so he looked up at me.

"I don't know. He was there when I went to sleep. I thought you had him too."

"Fuck!" I shouted.

"He will have gone back to Atlanta. He hasn't got anyone left here, and he'll be scared," Havana stated.

"Let's get this over with so we can find that nigga before he causes any more problems," my pops added.

Havana turned and shot Alonso straight in the head while Kymani lifted his Glock and hit both Zain and my mom within a second of each other.

"Yo Dre, get the crew in here to clean this mess up and take them over to the funeral home on West Madison," Kymani called out.

"Since when do we take bodies to the funeral home?" I asked.

"Since we bought that shit. It's a perfect cover. It's fire, literally," Ky said, laughing at his joke.

"I say we kill two birds with one stone and go to Atlanta. We can find this bitch ass A.J. and get Hallie back at the same time," I suggested on the way out the door.

"Have you thought about what you're going to do with her and Harvey once you get Hallie back?" my pops asked.

"Honestly, pops, I haven't really thought about it. I guess I'll just have them stay at the crib until they finish school, but I'm not on no fuckery shit. They both need to know that I'm not playing any games. I'll be there if they need me, but they need to know what kind of nigga I am these days. I'm not down for the bullshit. They either with me or against me, and it ain't nothing to me either way."

"Facts. I'll get the jet fueled up and ready to go. We've got three days until your ma's birthday, and we need to make that shit extra special, so we have to be back here by Thursday night."

"We got Havana back, and ma's still gonna want a present? Damn, these women," Kymani added, and we all laughed.

"I'm not fucking with ma like that right now, but you know I have to make it special for my main lady."

"Mama's boy," my pops teased while nudging me in the side.

22

______

HALLIE

Looking at the screen, I saw it was my grandma calling me for the tenth time today. I haven't heard a peep from her in almost six months. One day, we had a huge argument, which ended in me walking out of her house and coming to live with my man, Keys. I've ignored her calls all day, but now Keys has gone out, I don't see the harm in answering her call. In all truth, I missed my grandma, but it also might be important.

"Hi, grandma," I said sheepishly into the phone.

"Hallie, baby. I need your help. Your brother is missing, and he hasn't been home for weeks. I've tried all of his friends, but everyone is saying they don't know where he is. Harvey won't answer the phone for me, so I need you to phone him and check up on him. Please. I just need to know that he is safe."

"No worries, grandma, I got you. I'll phone you once I know something," I said, ending the call and instantly dialing my brother's number.

"Hallie, are you ok?" Harvey quizzed, answering on the second ring.

"Where the fuck are *you*, Harvey? Grandma is worried sick about you. You need to go home."

"That's a bit rich coming from you, Hallie. How about you come home, and everything can be ok again?"

"I've told you before that my home is here with my man," I added, irritated.

I've told them a hundred times that I'm not hearing what they have to say until they accept my relationship. Keys already hates my family and has stopped me from visiting them. It's not that he is trying to control me or anything, but I come home upset each time I go there. After the last time, he told me I was not to go back there until they could respect me. It's difficult for me not to see my family and I miss them a great deal, but as he keeps reminding me, he and the rest of the gang are my family now.

"That's not your family, Hallie. We are. That motherfucker Keys don't give a shit about you. Can he protect you when that nigga's Glock and goons come looking for you? The streets talk Hallie, and everyone knows Keys robbed that nigga's shipment. He put the word out that he'll pay a hundred bands for anyone who brings him Keys alive. When that didn't get immediate results, he said he would take you and Key's mama instead, knowing that would draw him out. I've been trying to contact you ever since it happened, but you never want to answer your phone. Let me ask you, how many times did grandma have to phone before you picked up?"

"Harvey, you're still a kid, so you don't know what it is to be in a real relationship. Keys is my priority, not you and grandma. Until you accept him, shit is just the way it is. Glock ain't gonna do shit with his old soft ass. That nigga's been out of the game for a minute, so he must've not heard that we are running the south side these days. His old ass can go back to wherever the fuck he's been at with all that talk."

"Hallie, are you that fucking stupid, or that nigga's dick just got your damn head gone? Glock ain't done shit but step back from the front line. That nigga still runs shit, and you're an idiot if you think Keys is gonna get one over on him and live to tell the tale," Harvey replied cockily, getting me heated quickly.

"You don't know what the fuck you are talking about, Harvey. Just get your ass home to check on Grandma. She's worried about you."

"How about you go fucking check on her, Hallie? I'm in Chicago, and I won't be home for a few days."

"What the hell are you doing in Chicago?" I snapped, knowing his ass better not have been with his cracked-out mama all this damn time.

"I'm coming to find Harlem if you must know. I need someone to help you see what you're doing is crazy, and at this point, he is the only person who will be able to save you from Glock."

"Fuck that nigga! He ain't shit! He left us and never even came for us! You do remember that don't you?"

"Since I've been here, everyone has been telling me the same thing. Dad kept him away from us. Harlem tried to find us, but Marlo told him he would go to the police if they ever showed up again."

"Well, you wasted your time 'cuz I ain't going anywhere with either of you. I don't know how many times I have to tell you. This is my family now!" I snapped back at him before ending the call.

I slammed the phone down on the table so hard that I just knew I'd cracked my screen. I jumped at the sound of the front door opening. Turning around quickly, I saw Keys staggering into the hall being supported by his friend Nines.

"Hallie, help me! He's been hit!" Nines called out.

I rushed over to help get Keys into the chair.

"What happened?" I asked while grabbing the first aid kit, alcohol, and clean towels. Sadly this is not the first time since we've been together that I've had to pull a bullet out of a wound.

"We were outside the trap, and someone rolled by and fired shots at us. Keys wouldn't let me take him to the hospital, but he's losing a lot of blood."

"Ok, let me look at it."

I pulled Keys' t-shirt over his head to see the damage. Taking the alcohol, I soaked a rag and started cleaning around the wound. I could tell that the bullet was still inside his arm.

"You have to get it out for me, baby. Use your eyebrow tweezers and pull it, just how I showed you before," Keys instructed.

Doing exactly as my man told me, I grabbed the pair of tweezers and opened up the hole until I could see the end of the gold bullet. I picked up a second, larger pair of tweezers and tried to pry the bullet out. Keys screamed out in pain and bit down on the towel I'd placed in front of him. Nines handed him some Henny, and he started drinking it straight from the bottle.

After a few minutes, I managed to retrieve the bullet from Keys arm. By the time I was finished, Keys had passed out. I don't know whether it was the pain or the half of a bottle of Henny that he just downed. Nines helped me to get him onto the sofa so that he could get some rest.

I walked back into the kitchen to finish tidying up.

Seconds later, Nines came into the room and took a seat at the table.

"Who did this?" I asked.

"I don't know, Hal, but what I do know is that they were aiming for Keys. There were five of us outside that trap, but he was the only one who got hit. Whoever did this has got to be some straight shooter, sis. This wasn't some normal drive-by. This was a fucking hit. Y'all need to be careful 'cuz as soon as word gets out that he ain't dead, they could come back and try to finish the job. I need to get out there and see what I can find out. I'll keep you updated. Lock all the windows and the doors, and don't open them for anyone," Nines warned.

The look on his face and the tone of his voice made a cold shiver run down my back.

"Do you think this was something to do with Glock?"

"Yeah, it could be, but I can't make a move until I have some proof. I told Keys that he never should've been up against him. Glock is a real fucking OG. Ain't no way he's gonna let that slide. Why do you think he made you drive that night? 'Cuz he was moving alone. We were all told to fall the fuck back, but Keys didn't listen. The boss is at his head over it, and he has caused problems within the family for going against a strict order, but you know what he's like. Keys just doesn't listen to anyone. You're in danger, Hallie, and I don't think that this life is really what you want deep down. You need to get out now, while you still can," he advised.

Nines gave me a quick hug and left the house.

I followed behind him and locked the front door before walking around the entire house and checking that all my windows and our patio doors were locked. My mind went straight back to my earlier conversation with my brother.

Harvey said the streets talk, but my stupid ass didn't think to ask what the fuck they were saying. Maybe if I wasn't so hard-headed, I could've stopped this happening to my man. I'm pretty sure that this was one of Glock's men. It's just too coincidental that Harvey said that Glock was on Key's ass, and then this happens. But then again, if Nines is right, and the order from higher up was that the gang were not allowed to make this move, then the threat could be closer to home. Keys completely ignored an order, and that is a disrespect that our OGs won't take kindly to, and more than likely, they will send someone close to him to pull the trigger. At this point, I don't know whom I can trust.

23

———

VEE

Ever since Havana has been here, we've hardly spoken to each other, and it's killing me. I have a million questions that I want to know the answers to, all the things that a mom should know about her daughter. I want to know everything, from her first memory to her first crush, her favorite color, song, and everything in between. My husband keeps telling me I have to give it time. Havana has just had her entire world turned upside down, and I should let her wounds heal before trying to bombard her with questions. I know he understands my pain to an extent, being that he didn't find out about Harlem being his son until he was fifteen. However, this is different from their situation. I grew this child inside me and have mourned her every day since. I swear, just thinking about it makes me wish I could bring Yayo's snake ass back from the dead to kill him all over again.

I am pleased that Liberty and Brooklyn have had more luck than I have with trying to make conversation with their big sister. It warmed my heart to watch them all enjoying themselves outside by the pool. I decided to order some food and join the four of them outside. Since my husband, Harlem, and Ky had left earlier to go to Atlanta, it was just Liberty, Brooklyn, Havana, Ashlee, and I here with four security team members. I ordered enough food for everyone and a couple more bottles of alcohol, hoping that would help to break the ice with my daughter.

I made a pitcher of rum punch and one of just fruit punch. I took them outside with some glasses and sat down on one of the loungers by the pool. They were playing around like they had known each other for a long time.

"I made some drinks for y'all. It's a rum punch and a fruit punch. Oh, and I ordered some food for everyone. It will be here soon," I called out, pouring myself a glass of rum punch.

Ashlee got out of the pool and came to sit down in the seat next to me. I poured her a drink and handed it to her.

"Havana will come around, you know. She's still in shock with everything that has happened these last few months. Soon it'll be like you were never apart."

We sat and spoke for a bit longer before being interrupted by one of the security men, who let me know that the food had arrived. Ashlee helped me lay all the food out on the table and grab the plates for everyone to eat. We made plates for all four of the security team, who took them back to their posts to eat, before sitting down at the table together with Liberty, Brooklyn, and Havana.

As we ate, the conversation flowed easily. Ashlee kept refilling our glasses and I was starting to feel a little tipsy. Not long after we finished eating, Brooklyn let us all know that he was going back inside so he could phone his girl-friend. She had initially been here with us, but she had gone home a few days ago. Liberty said she was going to do some coursework for school tomorrow, and also went back inside the house.

"I thought they would never leave! But now that they've gone, can I light this blunt Mama Vee?" Ashlee slurred, making us all laugh.

"Ash! You can't say shit like that. That's my little brother and sister!" Havana stated in all seriousness.

"The hell I can't! I know ma don't let us smoke when they are around and a bitch dying for a blunt. They know I love their little asses, but I love me a blunt with my punch too, bitch!"

WE ALL SAT AROUND TALKING, drinking, smoking, and laughing for the rest of the night. Within hours, we were talking like we were old friends. Havana was warming to me, and I planned on relishing in every single second. Before I knew it, it was one a.m., and I was drunker than a motherfucker. All I wanted to do was curl up in my bed, but I didn't want this night to end. I was relieved when Havana stood up and declared that she'd had enough to drink and was going to sleep.

We all went inside, making sure to lock the door behind us. Although I knew we had security guarding us and the house, I couldn't shake the uneasy feeling that came over me. I got myself a bottle of water out of the fridge and turned to walk up the stairs, but something outside caught my eye. I looked again, but there was nothing there.

I called out to Tony, the head of security for the night shift, and he came walking into the room. I told him that I thought I'd seen something outside, so he radioed the others and told them to walk around the house and check if there was anything there. He reassured me that if there were anyone out there, he would put the house in lockdown mode, which meant that none of the doors or windows could be opened until the alarm was turned off. Only myself, my husband, and Tony had the power to deactivate the alarm via an app on our phones that used an eye scanner.

I went up to my bedroom and waited for Tony to tell me if there was an issue. Within minutes, he had phoned me and told me that there wasn't anyone there, but as a precaution, he had arranged some additional security to join the four that we already had. I didn't want to worry any of the others, and I felt reassured that Tony could handle anything which may happen.

I propped myself up the bed and phoned my husband. I hated sleeping alone, especially this soon after we reconnected. He answered the phone on the first ring.

"Baby, is everything ok?" he asked, sounding concerned.

"Everything is fine. I just miss you, that's all."

"I miss you too. I promise, nothing will stop me from making it home for your birthday."

We spoke for a while longer before the sleep took over. I said goodnight to my husband and ended the call. Within minutes, I was sound asleep.

24

HARLEM

"We will be landing at Hartsfield-Jackson Atlanta in fifteen minutes," the pilot called out over the intercom on the G5.

The flight from Chicago had taken less than two hours, and I swear, it was the most comfortable seat my ass has ever been in. This was my first-time riding on a private jet, and I already knew it wouldn't be my last. This was goals, and you can bet your ass that I'd have myself one of these in a few years. I couldn't believe it when my pops told me that my uncle had bought this beast. This shit is fly as fuck. Just know that my ass will be going every damn where on this bitch.

I didn't want to leave Havana, but I've got to try to save my sister. I just hope she understands my situation, but I also hope she uses this time to get to know Mama Vee a little. I've told Havana that she needs to give her a chance. There is no way I can have my two main ladies not getting along. I could understand her hesitation if ma had just left her, but that good for nothing motherfucker Yayo lied to them both for all these years. I know it's hard when you first realize that one of your parents ain't shit, but there ain't shit we can do to change the past, but we damn sure can fix our futures.

Word has it that Keys got hit earlier today, and I know for a fact that it was a direct order from Glock. It was a warning shot, and I'm certain the next one won't miss. My dad has managed to get a sit-down with Glock tomorrow, and I can only hope that he is open to what we have to say regarding leaving Hallie out of this. Luckily for my sister, my dad knows Glock from back in the day, and so he's hopeful that he'll be able to get him to do a deal to keep Hallie safe. That's all I care about and all I came here to do. I won't speak for that nigga Keys. That dumb piece of shit made his choices, and he can live with the consequences. Little niggas are getting too brave these days. What the fuck was he thinking trying to fuck with an OG like Glock? It doesn't even make sense. I don't know this kid Keys, and already I know I don't like him. I just can't get along with stupid, and he sounds about as stupid as they come.

Don't get me wrong, I've wanted to have my brother and sister back in my life for the longest, but the timing couldn't be any worse. As a family, we've had a lot to deal with these last few months, and I could do without the extra pressure right now. Not only that, but since I made it official with Havana, nothing has gone right. I wanted to just spend time with my woman and get back to full health before I had to be out in the streets on bullshit like I am now. On the real though, I'm just happy to be alive and have my baby back by my side.

I've been thinking about Mya a lot too, so before we left for the airstrip, I phoned Tech and asked him to look into her. I just have to know the truth. I don't want to ruin what I'm trying to build with Havana, but I can't move forward without knowing what happened and if Mya was in on the plan to break my heart. I've been so angry at Mama Vee, but now my anger is directed at Mya and her parents. I always knew their stuck-up asses never liked me, but this is some straight-up bullshit. Who the hell fakes their own daughter's death just to get her away from her first love? That's some crazy shit that I just can't get my head around.

As soon as we touched down in Atlanta, we got the limo driver to take us to our hotel so we could check-in and grab some food. I needed to line my stomach for what I had planned for tonight. We were going to check out the famous King of Diamonds. I was officially celebrating being alive, and I had every intention of enjoying myself. I'm a one-woman man now, so this is the only way I'll be seeing any new ass or titties again, so I need to make the most of it.

As soon as we walked into the club, the DJ shouted over the mic.

"I swear my eyes must be playing tricks on me! I could swear I just saw that nigga Big H walk up in here! Aww, y'all ladies are going to make your rent money and some tonight!" he announced with a wicked laugh.

I turned to my pops, who was shaking his head and laughing. He raised his hand in the air, signaling to the DJ, who pointed back at him with a huge grin. The hostess came and escorted us up to the VIP area.

"Hey H, how are you tonight? I've got your table ready for you." She greeted my pops with a warm smile.

"Everything is good, thanks, Gloria. How are you and your kids?"

"Oh, we're good. You know them little boys are hard work, but they, my babies." She laughed as she pulled open the rope to our section. There were already four ice buckets on the table with different bottles sticking out of them.

My pops handed Gloria some money and thanked her. They made small talk for a minute before she left us to it.

"How the hell all these people know your, pops?" I asked, turning to face my dad.

"The crew and I be coming here occasionally," he answered sheepishly.

"Occasionally? Don't make me laugh, nigga. They all know your name, you've got your table, and they even know your drinks. You a fucking regular up in this bitch, and you couldn't even bring us with you, not one time?" Kymani voiced, pouring himself a glass of Henny.

"Ok, you got me, but don't tell your mama. Since your Uncle Rock got his jet a few years ago, we take a flight out here once a week on a Thursday. Your mama thinks it's a business meeting. Well, it's kind of is. It's team building," he joked with a laugh, grabbing the bottle from Ky and pouring himself a drink.

"Ky, it looks like we just got ourselves invited to these business meetings my pops be having every week. It's only right since we're a part of the organization, right, pops?"

"Yea, you know this spoiled little nigga will go running to his mommy and tell on us if we don't let him," Uncle Rock chimed in.

"Nigga, fuck you too, with your sneaky ass. You didn't tell us either."

We sat and enjoyed the rest of the night. It felt good to

be around close family and friends. I knew that tomorrow would bring its own set of problems, but tonight was all about having fun. We popped bottle after bottle and threw bands at these bitches for the next few hours before calling it a night and going back to the hotel.

25

HALLIE

Ever since Nines left here last night, I've been on edge. Keys only woke up to take some more pain meds before smoking a blunt and falling back to sleep. When he was awake, I tried to ask him who he thought had hit him and if he thought we were in any danger. He just brushed me off, as he always does. Keys is always telling me to grow up, but in the next breath, he treats me like a child. He only ever tells me what he thinks I need to know, but as recent events would show, I know nothing.

The night he asked me to drive for him, he said we were just collecting some money that was owed to him. He said it would only take five minutes, and then we could go out and enjoy ourselves for the rest of the night. Naively, I jumped at the chance since Keys was out with the crew or in the trap most evenings. I pulled up at a warehouse, and Keys got out. He told me to keep the doors locked and the engine running. The second I saw him approaching, I was to unlock the doors and drive off. I didn't realize what he was doing until he got out of the car and pulled the ski mask over his head.

Not even two minutes after Keys got out of the car, another car pulled up, and I saw Glock getting out and walking into the building. I waited for a few minutes. The nervousness swelled inside of me until I finally saw Keys running from around the side of the building. I unlocked the door, and I sped off the second he got in. I heard gunshots behind us as someone ran out behind him, shooting at us. I was so scared that I almost crashed into a row of parked cars.

"Concentrate, Hallie, for fucks sake!" Keys shouted at me, causing me to swerve again before regaining control of the car.

"You told me you were collecting money that was owed to you. You didn't mention anything about robbing Glock! What the hell are you thinking, Keys?"

"How many times I got to tell you not to question me? I'm the man in this relationship, and I suggest you learn that quickly, Hallie. You don't need to question me. You just need to know that I know what's best, so you need to do what the fuck I tell you to do."

I sat in silence, not knowing what to say to him. When Keys is in this mood, there is no point in me saying anything. It's best to just agree with him. It's the only way to avoid a fight. I know he is right, and I need to listen to him more. As he says, most of the arguments are my fault. It's always something I did or didn't do properly. I try so hard to make him happy, but the longer we're together, the worse his attitude gets.

Despite what I tell my family, life with Keys is not what I thought it would be. In the early days of our relationship, Keys was the nicest, most caring man I'd ever met, but in recent months that side of him has disappeared, and now he was controlling, possessive, and downright annoying. We fight now more than ever and don't get me wrong, I'll fight back, but he always overpowers me, and I come off worse every time. I'm unhappy most of the time, and it got to where I've been asking myself if this is what I want, but my hard-headed ass didn't want to hear anyone telling me that they told me so. With that in mind, I've been trying harder to make this relationship work, but I fear that in trying to keep Keys happy, I'm losing myself in the process.

Within minutes of being out of the shower, this mother-fucker was putting his sneakers on to leave the house

"Where are you going, babe? Don't you think you should rest?"

"No, I've got shit to do and moves to make. Stay here and don't leave the house. I'll come back later and get you, pack a bag cuz I'm taking you away for a few days."

"You don't even know who did this to you, Keys. You need to be careful."

"I'm always careful," he replied, kissing me passionately before turning and walking out of the front door.

Five minutes later, there was a knock at my door. I opened the app for the camera from my phone to see who was there. It surprised me to see my brother Harvey. I could've sworn this little nigga told me he was in Chicago. Knowing that Keys wouldn't be back for a few hours, I opened the door.

"We need to talk," he stated in a serious tone.

"I don't need to hear this shit right now, Harvey. What do you want?" I snapped, still not being able to admit that I had missed my little brother.

"Just open the door and stop being a bitch, Hallie. I'm not going anywhere until you hear me out." Feeling frustrated, I swung open the door and stepped back to let him in, closing the door behind him.

I led us to the kitchen and offered him a seat at the breakfast bar before pouring us both a drink. I took the seat next to him and stared at him. Although it was only seven months since I'd seen him, he's changed so much. He's turned from a boy into a man, and seeing his face makes me realize I've missed him more than I would ever let on.

"I thought you were in Chicago?" I started.

"We came back last night."

"We who?" I asked, just as his phone started ringing.

Harvey got up and walked out of the front door, so I couldn't hear what he was saying. While I waited for him to come back in, I picked up my phone and started scrolling. I saw a post about Keys getting shot outside the trap yesterday. In reading all the comments, my mind was so distracted that I didn't even notice Harvey returning to his seat. I looked up and almost jumped out of my skin when I noticed the four men that were also now standing in my kitchen.

"Harlem, what are you doing here?" I asked, relieved to see that it wasn't someone here to kill Keys or me.

"We've managed to come to a deal with Glock on your behalf. In exchange for him not killing you, you've got to leave Atlanta and not come back. You have twelve hours to make it over state lines, or he'll kill you. This isn't a joke, Hallie. My dad had to call in a favor to get him to agree to this. You can either come with us or go the fuck on, but either way, you're leaving. Hurry and pack your shit," Harlem explained.

"I'm not going anywhere with you. Keys is taking me away for a few days, so I'll be fine."

"I don't think you're listening, Hallie. You are leaving, one way or another. I'd rather you did it willingly. I don't have time for this bullshit. If you are still in Atlanta tonight, you'll be dead. It's that fucking simple, and I don't have time to go to war with the King of the A over some dumb shit that should've never happened. Is this motherfucker Keys worth losing your life over? You really are as stupid as your mama if you believe that nigga is worth the trouble he's caused. Now, I don't give a shit if you want us to have a relationship right now, but I'm not leaving you here to get murdered. Now, pack your shit!!!!" Harlem demanded, making sure to shout the last part, so I knew he was serious.

I didn't know what to do. I just looked from one of my brothers to the other, remembering a time when I ached to have my big brother back. I turned a bit more and scanned the other men. The only one I recognized was Big H. He was always so kind to us. The sound of a phone ringing grabbed my attention. I looked toward the man who had now answered the call. He turned around and said a few words into the phone before turning back to face Harlem and speaking.

"They've got eyes on him."

Big H nodded his head, then he turned to me.

"Glock's men found Keys using the tracker we put on his car last night. He won't get away with a warning shot like he did yesterday. Hallie, what we're telling you isn't optional. One way or another, you're leaving Atlanta tonight. Be my guest if you think you can make it out there alone. I'll break you off a lil' bread, and you can go on about your business. I will personally put your ass on the flight myself. Or you can come back to Chicago with us while you work out what you want to do next. This is your opportunity to build a relationship with your brother. I suggest you take it while you have the chance. He is recovering from shots that should've killed him. You don't have the time to sulk. You can do that when we make it back to the Chi. Just grab anything you need, and let's go. My wife's birthday is less than twenty-four hours away, and I have a whole damn party to plan. Let's wrap this shit up and go home."

Reluctantly, I went upstairs and started putting all of my belongings in bags. I took the small amount of money that I had managed to save and headed back down the stairs. As I walked into the room, something on the television caught my eye. A news reporter on the screen talked about gun violence in the city. Living in a place like this, you hear that shit on the news daily, but just as I went to switch the television off, the scene changed. I was looking at a car identical to Keys' but riddled with bullet holes.

"There was a shootout on the expressway just minutes ago, and we are live at the scene. Eye-witness reports say shots were being fired from the vehicle you see here, and another car involved in the incident. The driver of the car has been taken to the hospital and remains in critical condition. The driver of the other car has not been located, but police say they are looking for the other people involved."

I just broke down on the floor and cried. Harlem came into the room, noticing what was on the television, he pulled me up off of the floor and held me.

"Hallie, you know that what he did was stupid. He was acting reckless, but he didn't care enough about you to keep you out of it. He had to be taught a lesson. I know you're hurting right now, but you must learn from this too. It doesn't matter how bad you think your lil' gang is. There are always people bigger than you. Keys knew what he was doing was a suicide mission. His bosses had ordered him not to try to make a move on Glock. If he didn't kill him, someone else would've."

"You didn't even give him a chance," I sobbed into my brother's chest.

The others came filing into the room. Harvey picked up my bags, and Big H asked if I was ready to go. I just shook my head. I knew I wasn't ready to leave. How could I go anywhere without knowing that my man is ok?

"I just need to see him," I managed to get out between sobs.

The others all made their way to the car which was parked in the driveway. When I stepped outside, I noticed a car parked across the road. The man got out, and Big H walked toward him. I couldn't hear what was being said, but I watched as they shook hands, and the man got back in his car and drove away.

When we pulled off, Harlem turned to me. "That was Glock's right-hand man. He was outside your house to make sure you left. Had you refused to come with us, he would've killed you before I made it to the end of the street. This is not a game, Hallie. Glock is a real fucking OG. I don't know what the hell y'all were thinking."

As we stepped onto the plane, I was in awe. I've always dreamed about going on a private plane, but this shit is a different level of comfort. I wanted so badly to ask who's plane it was, but I stayed quiet. I pulled out my phone and launched my Kindle app. It opened right where I left off. Right now, the only way I won't lose my shit is to lose my mind in a book. Until I hear from Keys, I'll stay quiet, but the second my man is ok, I'll tell him to come and get me. I want us to move and start a new life away from everyone.

26

HAVANA

I sat in our bedroom, looking through all the paperwork from out of my dad's safe. I couldn't believe how many things I was now the owner of. I knew I would have to show my face at these businesses and check that everything was running smoothly, but I didn't have a clue where to start.

I took the pile of documents downstairs, hoping to find Vee. Over the last few days, we've been talking and getting to know each other. The more I speak to her, the more I hate my daddy for letting me grow up with a bitch like Ameena as my mother when my real mom is so kind and sweet. I have a whirlwind of emotions inside me, and unless I do something, I feel like I'm going to explode.

When I got downstairs, Vee was sitting at the breakfast bar working on her laptop. As soon as she saw me, her whole face lit up.

"Morning, baby, can I get you some breakfast?" she asked, motioning to the spread laid out on the sides.

"Thanks, I'll have some in a minute. I was hoping that you could give me some advice."

"Of course," she offered, pouring herself a glass of juice and sitting back down next to me.

"In the last call I had from my daddy, he told me I was to go inside his safe and take everything in there. When I looked through all the documents, I came across a letter from him. He admitted the truth about everything. I'm so hurt by his actions, but my heart is torn. I love my daddy so much, but I hate him at the same time." I stopped to compose myself because I didn't want to get emotional. I needed help.

"It's ok to be angry. Your dad hurt you, but I get it. He is also the man who raised you. Trust me. Only a man can make you love them and hate them in the same breath. Your dad wasn't all bad. He had his good points, well he used to."

"Apart from the letter, there were the deeds to all the businesses and houses. He left everything he owns to me. I have all the paperwork, but I have no clue what to do next. I was hoping you could help me."

"Of course. Can I see the paperwork?" Vee asked.

While she was reading it, I got up and made myself a plate of food. There was so much food laid out that it was like being at a buffet cart. I took a pastry and a bowl of fruit before pouring myself a glass of juice.

Listening to Vee speak, she made it all sound so easy, but I didn't have a clue what I was doing. Being that she and Harlem's dad owned many businesses, she knew her stuff. It made me realize that I would have to learn a lot if I wanted to make these businesses work to their full potential.

We sat around discussing business for the next couple of hours until Ashlee walked into the kitchen.

"It's so nice to see you two finally talking to each other," she noted as she came and took a strawberry from my plate. I swatted her hand away playfully.

"I was just asking for some advice on how best to deal with all of this stuff my daddy left me. I have to go through everything at some point, so I might as well make it today."

"How about we get ready, drive over to all the businesses, and show your face? You can make everyone aware of who you are and reassure them they'll have nothing to worry about as long as they are performing their jobs properly. We'll take a look at the books for each of the businesses, make sure that everything is running as it should be, and then go shopping for the rest of the afternoon," Vee suggested.

"That sounds good. Thank you," I said, smiling at her.

"Yes, I need to go shopping! Ky sent me an entire list of things that I have to pick up today, but *you* can't see any of them," Ashlee added, pointing at Vee with a massive grin on her face.

"What did I miss?" I asked, confused.

"Tomorrow is Mama Vee's birthday, and Ky is worried that they won't make it back in time to get everything they need, so I've been trusted to collect all of her presents from Kymani and Harlem. And they have warned me that she is not allowed to see anything."

"Oh my god! I didn't even know. I have to get you something," I voiced. I realized I don't know what Vee likes. I don't know her favorite flowers or even her favorite fragrance.

"My baby, you are the only gift I need. I've spent so many years wondering what kind of person you would be. Now that to have you here is like a dream to me." As Vee spoke, tears ran down her face.

I stood up and hugged her, and we both stood there crying. When I turned back to look at Ash, she was crying too.

"We have the rest of our lives together. I swear, I could

kill my dad, but I have a feeling that someone already beat me to it. He's never gone this long without calling me and A.J. and Alonso would never have kidnapped me if my dad had been here. Still, I can't think about all of that right now. We've got a birthday to plan!"

We all dried our tears and went off into our rooms to get ready for the day. Thankfully, I was starting to feel more like myself. The bruises had healed entirely, and the swelling had gone away. I decided to opt for some light makeup and pull my hair into a messy bun. I made a note to call and book an appointment with my stylist, as my hair is in serious need of some attention. I put on some booty-hugging jeans with a short top and my red bottom sneakers. I grabbed my Gucci shades and put them on my head.

WE LEFT in Vee's car with the security detail following behind us. Ashlee was still getting used to being followed, but I've had security around me my entire life. I wasn't allowed out alone until I was eighteen, so this is nothing new to me. I just hope it's not always going to be like this. My and Harlem's relationship has barely even begun, and already there has been nothing but drama.

Pulling my ringing phone out of my purse, a smile spread across my face seeing Harlem's picture on my screen.

"Hey, babe. Is everything ok? Did you manage to get through to your sister?"

"Yea, we're on the way home now. She's not happy about it, but it's tough shit. I should only be a couple of hours, but I need to get Hallie and Harvey situated, and there are a few things I have to do to make sure that everything is ready for ma's birthday tomorrow. Are you going to be okay for a few more hours?"

"Don't rush on my account. I'm fine. We're not even at the house right now. We're just going into the city. We're going to stop by the businesses my daddy left me so that mama can look over the books for me. Then we're going shopping. Luckily Ashlee told me about tomorrow. I can't believe you didn't mention it to me. How would I have looked without a gift, Harlem?"

"She'll have more than enough gifts from us, baby. That lady is spoiled as hell. I'm happy to hear y'all are out doing things together, but please tell me you didn't leave without your security detail?"

"I don't think I could've got away from them if I tried. I can't even take a shower without them wanting to know what I'm doing. I'm looking forward to seeing you later, though. Just text me if there is anything else that you want me to get while I'm out. I love you, Harlem."

"I love you, baby. See you soon."

27

MYA

I've had the strangest flashbacks after the run-in with the man while I was working at the hospital a few weeks ago. Although it doesn't feel like my life is flashing before me, that same man is in every scene that plays in my head. I keep feeling pain in my scars from where I was shot years ago. It's as if my body is trying to tell me something, but I can't work out what it is. When I ask my dad about it, he sticks to the same story I've been told all of these years. It's the same thing time after time. It's like he rehearsed what he was going to say to me when I asked, as the entire story stays the same, word for word.

Just over four years ago, I got shot in a random drive-by shooting by a bullet meant for someone else. When my mom died last year, I found some cuttings that she'd kept from the newspaper article about the shooting. There was no information. It just said that a young girl was killed after a shooting in the park. Witnesses said that a car drove by slowly and started shooting at the crowd and that an innocent young girl had lost her life. When I asked my dad, he said that one of my friends with me had sadly died from her injuries and that we were lucky that I survived.

I remembered nothing that happened before I woke up in the hospital bed with tubes and wires all over me. I thought it was strange that none of my friends ever came to visit me, but my parents said they had moved me away to Washington to be closer to the specialist surgeon who was treating me.

After the shooting, I was in such a bad way that I had to stay in hospital for almost a year while my wounds healed, and my body recovered. I used the time to continue my studies, and since I had no other distractions, for the most part, I managed to complete my medical degree in just under three years, and I'm now a second-year resident at the hospital where I had seen the man. The move was much to the annoyance of my parents, who hated the idea of me moving to Chicago. They tried everything to put me off when I was offered the placement, but I've worked so hard that there is no way I could turn it down. Eventually, when I was more established, I would move back to D.C. to be closer to my dad.

My memory was so limited that I didn't even remember any of my friends. I couldn't place any faces at all, but being here in Chicago felt familiar, which is weird as I'd never been here in my life until the week before my job started. I'd rented a small apartment near the hospital, making life much easier for me.

I hadn't thought about my life before the shooting. I've always just accepted whatever my parents told me as the truth. It was only now that I was questioning everything that I'd been told, and I had a feeling that the man at the hospital had the answers that I needed.

I went through my computer to find Havana's details,

and it appears that she was due to come in for a check-up last week, but she missed the appointment. *Bingo!* That can be my excuse for contacting her. I picked up the phone and dialed her number.

"Hello, is this Havana Garcia?"

"Yes, speaking. Who is this?"

"Oh, lovely. Havana, it's Dr. Tia Grayson. I see on my system that you were due to come in for a check-up last Tuesday, but you didn't come. Is everything ok?"

"I'm so sorry. It completely slipped my mind."

"I can re-schedule the appointment for you if you'd like. It would be wise just to get checked over and make sure that you're healing from your wounds. I have an opening on Monday. Shall we say eleven a.m.?"

"Yes, thank you. I'll see you on Monday at eleven," she replied politely before ending the call.

Now I just had to hope that she brought her boyfriend with her. The way he acted that day at the hospital, I know he is sure that he knows me. At first, I just thought he was mistaken, but then when his friend came and called me the same name, I knew there had to be more to it than just a strange coincidence. Something about the man is so famil-iar, and the more I keep seeing him in my flashbacks, the more confident I am that we know each other, and now, more than ever, I need someone that knows me before the shooting. I just hope that he can give me some information about who I was.

28

VEE

I t's my birthday, I'm excited to celebrate with my
family, but it will be even more special this year. Don't
get me wrong. My husband always goes extra hard to
make my birthday special for me, but having my daughter
back is everything to me, and after the year that this family
has had, we deserve a celebration.

I lay in the bed with my head on my husband's chest,
feeling like the luckiest woman alive. We were finally back
in our happy place, and I was going to cherish every
moment of it, 'cuz with the way our lives are set up, something could blow up any second and ruin it all for me. I can't
wait until he is fully legit and out of the game for good. The
streets are no place for a man of his age. He needs to step
back and let Harlem and Kymani take over. I want us to
enjoy ourselves, and now that Liberty was at college and
Brooklyn was in his last year at school, we're free to live a
little. Our kids are all practically grown. Even Brooklyn only
spends half the time at home because he is with his girlfriend so much.

There was a point earlier in the year that I didn't think

we would make it this far. In all our years of being married, we've never stepped out on our relationship. The only reason my husband has a leg to stand on right now is that I knew I'd lied to him for years. Because of my lies, I felt like I wasn't in a position to get too mad. That was my guilt speaking, though, and looking back, this motherfucker was lucky I didn't shoot him in the ass.

Just because a bitch forgave him, it sure as hell doesn't mean I've forgotten what he did or that I've forgotten that little bitch Imani is due a visit. With everything that has happened recently, she's gotten a slide a bit longer. My husband thinks I don't know that she has been trying to reach out again, and I'll give him his props. He has rejected all her advances. I just need to be sure that the rejection will continue now everything has calmed down. I have the address to her office, and she is gonna have to see me about the constant disrespect.

Realizing that I was awake, my husband pulled me close and nestled his face into my hair.

"Happy birthday, baby. I can't wait for you to see your gifts. You know my ass has got a lot to make up for this year, so you're being extra spoiled today."

"Aww, thank you, babe, but you know you didn't have to do all that," I replied, sitting up so I could straddle my man.

I could feel him getting hard just from the heat of my box. I leaned down and kissed him passionately. Even with morning breath, he was the sexiest man I've ever laid my eyes on.

Big H picked me up and carried me to our bathroom in one swift movement. He sat me on the counter while he turned the hot water on in the shower. We both stood in front of the mirror brushing our teeth, and I couldn't take my eyes off him. He is still as beautiful to me as the day we met, and he doesn't look like he has aged at all in that time apart from the few lines which have appeared next to his eyes.

"Stop staring at me like I'm a snack," he said jokingly.

"You've never been a snack, baby. You're the full meal," I corrected before stepping into the shower.

I soaped up the washcloth and started washing Big H's body, paying extra attention to his rock-hard dick. Just looking at that thing makes my mouth water. After all the years we've spent together, I still find my husband incredibly sexy, and he still turns me on in the worst way.

He picked me up so that my back was against the shower wall and kissed me deeply. We made love under the stream of hot water for the next hour until I heard someone banging on the door to our bedroom.

"Come on, we better get ready and go downstairs. I'm sure the kids are all excited to start your birthday cele-brations."

"I don't know if all of them will be. Harlem has barely said two words to me since he woke up. I don't know if he will ever forgive me for what happened to Mya."

"Harlem loves you as if you birthed him. Trust me when I tell you he'll get over it. On the other hand, Mya's family now they might have a problem. It makes no sense that they would fake her death just to get her away from a boyfriend they didn't like. They were always on different paths, but it didn't matter then. They were kids. They never would've lasted, anyway. It was puppy love, and it would've come to an end on its own without them having to break our son's heart in the process. I just hope that finding out that Mya is alive doesn't affect the relationship he is building with Havana. They are well suited, and they are clearly very in love."

"We need to look into this Mya thing a little more because of the way she acted when she saw Harlem. I don't know if she even remembers anything from before she was shot or if she is just a good actress. Either way, we need to get to the bottom of it and let him get the closure that he needs. I knew I should've hit those bitch ass parents of hers in the hospital that night."

"Come on, killa, let's go downstairs. We'll talk more about this later. Today is all about you," Big H relayed just as there was another knock on the bedroom door.

"Come in," I called out just as I finished brushing my hair.

"Happy birthday, ma, now come on. Everyone is waiting for you," Liberty excitedly said as she hugged me.

The three of us made our way downstairs to find the others.

Havana and Ashlee were cooking breakfast, while Harlem and Ky sat at the breakfast bar deep in conversation, and Liberty, Hallie, Harvey, and Brooklyn were all sitting at the table, laughing over a video on Brooklyn's phone. As soon as they saw me, they all started singing happy birthday. It was the best feeling ever. Although Kymani and Ashlee aren't ours, they used to spend so much time at our house that they feel like our kids too, but it is incredible to have all four of my children in here with me.

Every single occasion in my life, I've always wished my Heaven were with me, and now she is here where she belongs with her family. Not to mention, there was a time not so long ago that I thought my relationship with my stepson was over, and that broke my heart, but to see him sitting here front and center, surrounded by gifts, I know he is starting to forgive me. Having Hallie and Harvey back in

his life will make him so happy. I swear I feel like the luckiest woman alive right now, and nothing will ruin my day.

THE REST of the morning was spent enjoying the feast
cooked by Havana and Ash and me being showered in gifts.
Once everyone was finished, my husband announced that
he had booked all of us ladies for an afternoon of
pampering at my favorite salon, Exquisite Beauty. Tiana and
Neeka do their thing, and I just know I'll walk out of there
feeling and looking like a million dollars.

29

BIG H

After having the ladies picked up in a limo to get taken for their pamper session, we had to get everything in place for Vee's party tonight. All of our friends were coming out to celebrate with us, and I couldn't wait to see her face when she saw everyone. Even some of our old friends from New York had flown in late last night to be here with her today. It's not every day you turn forty, and I wanted to make it a birthday that Vee would remember for the rest of our lives. The past year has been the most fucked up year of our marriage, so the fact that she is still by my side means everything to me. Vee gave me the world when she had my babies and gave me a real family for the first time in my life, and the way she loves Harlem like he is her child shows the kind of woman that she is, so it's only fitting that she is treated like a queen.

The only problem I have right now is that Imani won't stop messaging and calling me. I've told her a hundred times that I love my wife and what we had was a mistake, but you know how these crazy bitches get. Today is the worst day for me to deal with all of this shit, but I need to make her understand I am not the one to keep fucking with.

I told the boys that I had an errand to run and gave them a list of things I needed them to do for the party this evening. That should keep them busy for a few hours, which is more than enough time for me to meet Imani at her office to shut this shit down once and for all.

The second I walked into the office. I just knew that Imani was on some bullshit. I wish I'd brought someone with me now because if I get caught here with her looking the way she does, I know my wife will shoot my dick off. Imani came walking from around her desk, wearing nothing but her lingerie and a pair of red bottoms.

"For fucks sake, Imani, will you put some clothes on! I didn't come here for all this bullshit. You said you had something important to talk to me about, which apparently you couldn't discuss over the phone. You've got five minutes, so get to talking." I put my hand up to stop her from getting any closer to me.

"Why are you being like this? I thought you enjoyed what we have?"

"We have nothing. We had sex a few times, but that's it. I never led you on or made you think it would be more than what it is, so I don't understand why you're acting all crazy now. Just tell me what it is you want to say."

"The police are looking into you again. After their witness didn't turn up to testify, they have not been able to track him down. They think he is dead and that you killed him. Do you know anything about it?

"If they are looking into me, why haven't they asked pulled me in for questioning yet?"

"I've managed to hold them off so far, but I don't know how much longer I can do that for."

"If they had any evidence, they would've arrested me by now. They don't even know for sure that he is dead. I'm not even worried, I know I had nothing to do with it, so they can't tie me to it."

"You know that anything you tell me is confidential. You can tell me if it was you who killed him. It is a bit odd that he disappeared right before giving evidence, and his own family hasn't even seen him. His wife and daughter have both reported him missing, and they've been making a lot of noise at the precinct due to the lack of help they are getting in finding him."

Imani almost had me believing her lies until that last part about his wife and daughter. If she knew like I knew, then she would know that his wife was cut into pieces and floating down Lake Michigan, and his daughter hadn't once mentioned to Harlem or Ash that she is searching for him. Since she's been back, she hasn't been anywhere alone, so I damn well know that Imani is lying. I knew what I would have to do, but it wouldn't be as easy as making her disappear. She is well known due to her job, so I know people will look for her.

"Ok, I'll come back to discuss my options, but today is not the day."

"When will I see you? What is so important that you can't stay now and talk?" Imani replied, trying to sound sexy and reaching for my chest.

"I've got some family stuff to sort out today. Let's talk tomorrow," I suggested, touching her face and pushing a strand of hair behind her ear. "I promise, clear your schedule for the entire day, and we'll spend the time discussing this case, and then I'll make up for not coming to see you more."

"Ok, I'll meet you at my house in the morning. Don't make me come looking for you," Imani warned, putting her hand on her hip with an attitude.

"I'll be there bright and early," I said, kissing her jaw.

I turned around and went to leave her office, but as soon as I walked back out into the reception area, I knew I'd fucked up. My wife was standing right by the reception desk, with Havana and Ashlee. When she heard the sound of shouting, Imani came walking out of the office behind me in her underwear.

"Vee, I promise, this is not what you think. I came here 'cuz she said she had to speak to me urgently regarding my case. I had no idea she wouldn't be dressed when I got here. I promise you, nothing happened."

"Imani?" Havana said from behind my wife.

"How do you know this bitch?" my wife asked, turning to Havana.

"Imani was one of my daddy's girlfriends. She's been with him for years."

With that, Vee charged at Imani.

"You bitch! You were setting him up all along?" Vee reined punch after punch down on Imani. It was like watching a professional boxer the way she was throwing them lefts and rights.

Imani was on the floor begging me to help her. After letting my wife take out some of that built-up aggression, I lifted her off of Imani, but the anger boiling inside her made her strong, and I struggled to keep hold of her.

"*They* are responsible for killing your dad, Havana. He was helping the police to try to get charges brought against Big H, but he disappeared before he could give evidence. I hadn't seen or heard from them since before *he* got out. You know your dad never goes more than a day or two without speaking to me," Imani said, pointing back at me with a tear-stained face.

"If you live by the sword, you die by it. My daddy knew better than to speak to the police, so if what you're saying is right, then he deserved whatever happened to him. Snitches don't last long in the streets, Imani. You should know that better than anyone," Havana replied before joining her mom in beating Imani's ass.

"Get out of my city, Imani. I'm not playing with you. If I ever see your face again, I will fuck you up," I warned, pulling my wife and Havana off Imani's prone body.

The second we walked outside. Vee punched me straight in the head and slapped me with the other hand just for good measure. I rarely play about all that fighting with my woman bullshit, but I knew I had it coming from the second she caught me there, so I took it like a G.

"You stupid ass motherfucker! We agreed, no more secrets. How dare you do this to me again and on my fucking birthday of all days?"

"I'm sorry, I should've told you. Why aren't you at the salon?"

"A few of Ti's girls went off sick today, so we left Lib and Hallie there to get started. I told her we would be back in an hour. Don't think I didn't see the fact that this little whore has been messaging you again, so I came here to tell her to back off before she gets fucked up. I swear to you on every-thing I love that bitch better be dead by the end of the day, or I'll kill you myself for playing with me. Get it done, Harlem!" she spat before turning on her heels and walking away like a boss.

It turns me on so much when my wife bosses up like she

just did. I know I have until midnight to make sure Imani is dead, 'cuz ain't no way I'm ready to fight my wife over this. What my queen wants, she gets. I made the call to seal the deal for Imani and drove away.

HAVANA

After getting in the limo that Big H sent for us, we sat back and enjoyed a glass of champagne while being driven to the salon. I've been meaning to book an appointment with Neeka to get my hair done since I came back. I know she'll get me right. I can't believe that I've been going to the same salon as my birth mom for all these years, and we never crossed paths. It is a small world sometimes.

When we got inside of Exquisite Beauty, the salon owned by my stylist Neeka and her sister Tiana, it was packed, and they looked to be rushed off their feet.

"Hey ladies, Happy birthday Vee. It's so good to see you." Tiana greeted us, hugging Vee like they were old friends.

"Hey, Ti baby, thank you. I've got the whole family with me today. These are my daughters, Liberty and Havana, Ky's girlfriend Ashlee, and Lil' Harlem's little sister, Hallie." Vee introduced us all.

"I already know Havana, but it's nice to meet the rest of y'all. Have you decided on what you would like to get done today, ladies? Big H insisted y'all treat yourselves to whatever you want, and he'll settle the bill at the end. Two of my ladies have gone off sick today, so as you can see, it's a little wild in here this morning, but I promise, you'll have my undivided attention within the next hour."

"Lib and Hallie, go and choose your hair, then you can get started. I'll take these two with me to give Tiana a bit of time, and we'll come back in an hour."

Vee led Ashlee and me outside and back into the limo.

"I've just got a quick stop I need to make. That lawyer bitch has been messaging my man again, and I need to go and put a stop to her shit. She's gonna learn today."

"Oh shit, I just knew you would get my ass in trouble." Ashlee joked. She's always for the shit.

I listened as they spoke about some lawyer that Big H had been fucking with while I was in the hospital. Ashlee's crazy ass doesn't need to be encouraged, so I feel that her and Vee mixing will only end in trouble for us all.

THE SECOND THE limo pulled up outside the office, we all jumped out and went inside the building. I was surprised to see that the entire reception area was empty. Just as Vee turned to look at us, Big H came walking out of one of the offices at the back. He looked like a deer in the headlights when he saw us standing by the vacant reception desk.

I didn't know what to think when Imani came running out of the office behind him in her underwear. She looked so smug when she saw Vee as if she enjoyed every minute of what she saw. I tolerated Imani for this long because she seemed to make my daddy happy, but she's just a home-wrecker who thrives on the bullshit. I played it off when she said they were responsible for killing my daddy, just like he taught me — never let anyone see your hand. I couldn't help myself after that. All the pent-up anger and aggression just came flying out.

WE GOT BACK to the salon an hour later and spent the rest of the day being pampered. It was just what I needed. I tried to zone out and enjoy myself, but I couldn't shake Imani's words. Nothing I do at this point will ever bring my daddy back, but if I look into this too much, I might not like what I find. *Am I ready to fuck up my future with Harlem over something I can't change and potentially ruin my relationship with the mother I just found?* I don't know what to do right now, and I wish I had someone I could turn to for advice, but the only people I have in my life are all connected in one way or another. I'm going to have to suck it up for the rest of today at least. It's Vee's birthday, and I'm going to smile and play my part, but tomorrow, I've got some hard decisions to make.

31

HARLEM

Ever since I woke up from being shot, I haven't had a single minute alone. I feel like I'm being ripped in ten different directions at once. All I want to do is take Havana and disappear, but I have to make sure Hallie and Harvey are both ok first. I can't just leave them. It's crazy how I'm still programmed to put their needs before my own.

I'm taking them out for the day so we can reconnect and discuss what's going to happen next. I'm also flying in their grandma. I've rented a house for them all to stay in. From what Harvey has been telling me, the old lady isn't in good health and seeing as they aren't going back to Atlanta any time, I phoned and explained the situation to her, and she is happy to relocate for a while. I asked Havana to come with us, but she said she had plans with Ashlee. Ever since coming back from the salon the other day, she has been distant. I just need a couple more days to get some shit in order, and I'm taking her on vacation anywhere in the world she wants to go.

I spent the entire morning shopping with Hallie and Harvey. I wanted to make sure they both had everything they needed. After spending racks at the mall, we stopped off to get pizza. When they were younger, this was their favorite thing to eat if they had the choice.

Hallie was starting to come around to the idea of being here, and she seemed to be getting used to life without that waste of space nigga Keys. I know it's only been a few days, but she has settled in well and is getting along with everyone, especially Liberty. Word on the street is that Keys died in hospital not long after being shot, although his injuries weren't the cause of his demise. As the police were changing shifts, someone went into his room dressed in scrubs and injected him with a lethal dose of morphine. His death was announced before we even touched down in Chicago.

AFTER WE FINISHED EATING, we went to collect the old lady from the airport and drove over to the house that I'd rented them. It's fully furnished and has a state-of-the-art security system which covers the entire house and gardens. I chilled with them for a couple more hours before heading home. I couldn't wait to get my ass in the crib and lay up with my girl.

An hour later, I made it back to my crib. I was happy as hell to be back home from the lake house. I enjoyed being able to walk around butt-ass naked if I choose to, and I can't do that if the entire family is under one roof. I called out for Havana, but there was no answer. Going from room to room, she was nowhere to be found.

Picking up my phone, I dialed her number. The phone repeatedly rang until the voicemail kicked in, I ended the call and phoned the number straight back, but the same thing happened. I phoned Ashlee to see if they were still together, but she said she had dropped her off at the crib hours ago. Straight away, I started to panic and think something bad had happened to her. I decided to go over to my parent's crib and see if any of them knew where she was.

WALKING INTO THE HOUSE, everyone was sitting around the table eating dinner.

"Ma, have you seen Havana today? She was with Ash, but she said she dropped her off hours ago, and she's not answering the phone."

"I spoke to her on the phone at lunchtime, but nothing since. Let me try to call her again."

Mama Vee picked up her phone to call Havana, but again it rang until the voicemail kicked in.

"I'm getting worried now. After recent events, she should know not to disappear like this. She could be fine, but I'm scared she's been kidnapped again. Shit, what if A.J. came back for her? Man, we have to find her. If something has happened to her again, I swear, I'll never forgive myself," I stated as I took a seat.

"Son, you can't think like that every time she's MIA for a minute. You'll drive yourself crazy. Have you checked your cameras? You'll see if anyone took her from the house."

"Good thinking, pops," I replied, taking my phone out and opening the app for my home security system.

Each camera in the house is linked and can be controlled through an app on my phone. It also controls the alarm system and key codes for the doors. I scrolled back through the footage of the front door until I saw Ashlee's car pull up in my driveway. They sat and spoke for a minute before Havana went into the house alone. Everything looked normal after I followed her movements through the house. I watched as we went from room to room, making sure everything was tidy, putting things away, and wiping the sides down. I watched as she entered our bedroom and left out fifteen minutes later with a small sports bag. She looked nervous as she waited by the door for her Uber to pull up. I watched as she looked back at the house before getting into the car and disappearing down the street.

"She left."

"What do you mean she left?" Mama Vee asked.

"She took a bag, got in an Uber, and left. Nobody took her. She walked out of the door herself."

"Something doesn't add up. Why would she just leave?" Liberty asked.

"I don't know, but we'll find her. I'd like you both to clear the table, please, and let us speak to your brother in private," my pops requested.

Once they did as he instructed, my pops started talking.

"Harlem, listen. There is something we should've told you the other day. Do you know that lawyer bitch? Well, she's been messaging me again, so I confronted her and told her to stop. When I walked out of the office, your mama was standing in the reception area with Havana and Ash. I don't know why her ass thought it would be a good idea to bring them with her, but she was ready to fight. It turns out that this Imani bitch was one of Yayo's girlfriends, and she was trying to set me up the whole time. She told Havana that we're responsible for killing her dad."

"Fuck! Why didn't anything think to tell me this? I just knew that this would come back to bite me in the ass. I have to find her. I have to explain."

I jumped up and ran out of the house, got in my car, and

sped off. I was so pissed off right now. I called out to Siri to phone Ky.

"Bro, she's gone. She fucking left me! I need a drink. Meet me at the club," I relayed before ending the call.

I pulled up on the side of the road and lit the blunt I had in the ashtray. I sat watching the taillights of the cars passing me, listening to the sound of the heavy rain, feeling lost. *Why am I never just allowed to be happy? What have I ever done that's so bad that my entire life is cursed?* I made a few phone calls to try to track Havana down. Although part of me thinks I should just leave her and let her be happy, I can't just let her go without even trying. I finished the blunt and continued the drive to the club.

WHEN I GOT THERE, the line was going halfway down the block. I parked right outside in my designated spot and walked straight into the club. I stopped to speak to a few of the security guards before walking over to the bar and grabbing a bottle of Henny. I then headed straight up to my office, where Ky was already waiting.

"What the fuck you mean she just left? Ashlee said Havana was fine when they were out earlier, and she's been trying to phone her too, but she's not answering anyone. Are you sure she's ok and her brother didn't come back for her?"

"Havana knows we killed her dad, and I think that's why she left."

"How the fuck did she find that out? Please don't tell me you told her."

"Do I look like an idiot? Of course, I didn't fucking tell her!" I snapped. "Didn't Ash tell you where they all went the other day when they asses should've been at the salon?

Mama got them, girls, acting stupid, and she's the one old enough to know better," I fumed.

"Ashlee knows better than to be out there on some dumb shit, and I don't care if it is your mama. Vee is a bad influence on Ashlee. Ashlee's dumb ass has been following Vee around that lake house for weeks like her little protégé in training. What stupid shit have they been doing now?"

"Mama took them to beat the brakes off the lawyer chick pops was caught fucking with. It turns out the bitch was Yayo's main side piece, and Havana knows her. She told her everything. Havana knew and didn't say shit to me. Even at home she acted like everything was normal, then she just left a nigga without a word."

"She'll be back. Tech is tracking her phone and her bank accounts as we speak. As soon as she makes a call or pays for something on her card, we'll have her location."

"I knew it would never work out for us. There has always been too much stacked against us. From the day we met, shit started fucking up in her life. Part of me wishes I'd never gone to the block party that night, and all of this bad shit would never have happened to Havana. How can she ever love me knowing I am the reason for much of the hurt in her heart?" I relayed, drinking the glass of Henny.

"I can't sit here and listen to you feeling sorry for yourself. Fix your mouth with all that bullshit you talking bro. Granted, y'all killed her whole family, but it's not like you had a choice. You also opened Havana's eyes to the snakes that were around her. Her 'mom' was fucking that old ass boyfriend of hers. Her dad is a fucking snitch who would've been killed by someone eventually, and her dumbass brothers are so fucking stupid they robbed three empty traps. Because of you, Havana knows who her real mom is and can move forward with her life. She loves you, Harlem.

Just give her time to get her head around everything that's happened, she'll come back, or she won't, but you'll be good whatever the outcome. On a different note, what's happening with this Mya situation? That shit needs to be looked into and put behind you."

32

HAVANA

Ever since I saw Imani the other day, her words have been playing over in my mind, and I just can't seem to shake the thoughts running around in my head. I swear to God, I have never felt so alone in my entire life. I can't even speak to Ashlee about it, as she is close to them all. Just when I thought things were starting to look up for me, that bitch Imani dropped a bombshell. I finally had Harlem back and a real mom with a normal family, or so I thought. I guess every family has skeletons in their closets, but this family may have more than most.

When I made the choice to leave Harlem's house earlier today, I wasn't thinking straight. I was so mad that I couldn't see past the hurt I felt, but now I've calmed down a bit, and I know that I should've allowed Harlem to explain his side of the story.

I've been sheltered from the street shit my entire life, but I know that had the roles been reversed, my daddy would've killed the person who was snitching on him too, so part of me can't blame them for wanting him dead, but he was still my daddy, and no matter what anyone says about him, that shit hurts. In the last six months, my world had gone crazy, and my daddy, the man I held on such a pedestal my entire life, was not the man I thought he was. I mean, it takes a special kind of fucked up to pull the stunt that he pulled on my mother. What kind of person fakes their own child's death in a bid to hurt an innocent mother?

My phone has been ringing back-to-back, but I'm not in the mood to speak to anyone right now, I know I should at least let them know that I am safe, but I can't be bothered by the hundred questions that will surely follow and nor am I in the mood to be lied to. I decided to go to the store over the road from the hotel and get myself some alcohol and snacks. Then I planned to get drunk and eat ice cream while watching old movies for the rest of the night. I'm just going to switch off from the world.

A BANGING on my hotel room door woke me out of my sleep. I checked the clock, and it was two-thirty a.m. I grabbed my nine, walked to the door, and slowly pulled it open. The second I did, it came flying open, and in walked an angry, very drunk-looking Harlem.

"So, after everything we done been through, you're just going to leave without a fucking word? Are you serious with me right now, Havana? If something was bothering you, you should've spoken to me. I promised I would always keep it one hundred with you, but obviously, you can't do the same for me."

"I needed some time to clear my head. I know I should've said something, but I'm angry. Y'all killed my dad Harlem. How the fuck am I supposed to feel?"

"I planned on telling you, but I just haven't had the

chance with everything that's happened. I'm sorry for hurting you, but you have to know why I did what I did," he slurred.

"I know already. He snitched on your dad and could've got him sent down for a long time."

"That's not the only reason. At the time, I didn't even know Yayo was your dad, and by the time I did, it was too late. We'd already kidnapped him by then, so I could hardly let him go. After Mya died, or when I thought she was dead, I was like a shell of my former self. I was heartbroken, and I spent the best part of three years trying to find the person responsible for shooting her. When I got back to where we were holding him, Mama Vee was already there. They were arguing, and he admitted it was him who shot Mya. He was aiming for Vee, but he missed and hit Mya instead."

"She came and shot him in the driveway to our house. I was in the car asleep, and I thought I was dreaming about it, but the next day when I saw how badly he was injured, I couldn't believe it. Her face, it just came back to me, it was Vee who shot him."

"I know you love your dad, but he hurt too many people. The person you knew is not the same person the rest of the world saw when they looked at him. He was an evil man who did a lot of bad things to a lot of people. I'm sorry, Havana, but he deserved what happened to him."

"Don't you think I know that? I know he deserved what happened to him, but he was still my daddy. Y'all took him before he even had the chance to explain his actions to me. I'll have to go through the rest of my life without ever knowing why he did the things he did. I don't know if I can be with the person responsible for that. I just need time to work out what I want, and I need to do it without you around me. I suggest you take this time and deal with this

Mya issue because if I come back, it's a wrap for holding onto the past," I cried.

Harlem came to my side and held me while I cried. My heart is torn into pieces, and the only person who can make me feel better is the same person who is responsible for the hurt to begin with. When he kissed me, I let him. I needed to feel the comfort of his arms, even if it would be the last time.

Starting slow and sensual, Harlem's kisses became passionate and urgent. He lifted me, and I wrapped my legs around him while he raced to free his huge dick. Gently gliding me up and down, he used my juices to wet his dick enough to slide it inside me. His thrusts were getting rougher as he held onto my ass while bouncing me up and down on his rock-hard dick. He was fucking me like he had a point to prove, and boy was he proving it. He made me cum back-to-back before falling back onto the bed and letting me ride him into another orgasm.

Within seconds of exploding inside of me, he was snoring. I got up to get a hot towel to wipe Harlem down before getting into the shower. I washed off quickly and got ready for bed. I climbed into the bed next to Harlem and felt peace when he enveloped me in his big, powerful arms. Sleep still didn't come easily to me, and I spent the next two hours trying to understand what the fuck happened to my life in such a short space of time.

33

HARLEM

I woke up confused as hell and felt like my head would explode. Wiping my eyes, I tried to look around and figure out where the fuck I was. I tried to sit up, but the pain in my head made me want to be sick. My eyes started to focus, and I saw Havana sitting on the sofa on the other side of the suite, scrolling on her phone.

"Where are we?"

"We're at a hotel. You tracked my phone and followed me here. I've thought about what you said last night, but I still need some time. I have a hospital appointment this morning, and I'd like it if you weren't here when I get back."

"Let me take you to the hospital. I need to go there and speak to Mya. I need some answers, and I want you to be there so that you know I'm not hiding anything else from you. I know you say you want space, but we still have a lot to talk about. The jet will be waiting for us tonight. I was going to surprise you and take you away somewhere, seeing as our last trip got canceled when your brother shot me."

"Fine, but hurry and get ready. I'm leaving here in ten minutes."

I rushed to get up and gather my clothes before heading to the shower. I was washed up and back out within eight minutes, but Havana was gone when I walked back into the room. This woman will make me mess around and kill her ass if she keeps running from me.

Walking outside the hotel, I got into my car and drove toward the hospital. The sound of my phone ringing snapped me out of my thoughts. I looked at my screen and saw a call from a number that I didn't recognize. I answered the call and listened as the person spoke.

"You stay the fuck away from my daughter. You and your family are nothing but dope dealing, gang-banging motherfuck-ers. I will destroy everything you and your family have. Your legal and illegal businesses will be ruined. I went to the ends of the earth to get her away from you once, and it'll be over my dead body that you will get close to her again. Leave them alone."

The bastard ended the call before I could even get a word in, but I knew without a doubt that it was Mya's dad. That old motherfucker is playing with the wrong one. He must not remember, but I'm not the same little kid I was when I was with Mya, and I don't take kindly to people who threaten my family or my livelihood. He wants it to be over his dead body, then so be it. He could be dead by sundown, playing with a thug nigga like me.

I PULLED up to the hospital feeling heated. I probably should've tried to calm down before going up in here, but they've all got me fucked up. Between dealing with Havana and her emotional, over-the-top ass, I've not gotten a chance to get to the bottom of this shit with Mya once and for all. She can play all the games she fucking likes. I'm not hearing any of that. You *have the wrong person* bullshit from her mouth today. She better tell me what the fuck happened.

I walked straight to the reception desk and asked to see Dr. Grayson.

"Are you a relative?"

"What a fucking stupid question to ask me. I thought people came to the hospital to see a damn doctor, and she *is* a doctor, right?"

"I'm sorry, sir. The doctor told me she was expecting a family member to arrive. She's not working today, but if you want to leave a message, I'm sure she will speak to you when she returns to work."

"So, she's here? I need to speak to her, it's important. Will you just go and get her?" I ran my hands over my head in frustration.

"I'll see if she has a minute. Could you take a seat, please?"

I went and took a seat in the waiting area. Two minutes later, the same receptionist came walking over toward where I was seated.

"Sir, you can go back. She's in room number 435."

"Thank you," I replied politely and walked through the double doors that led to the private rooms.

I walked along the hallway until I spotted the room number. I stopped outside and peered through the glass. Seeing that Mya was in the room, I walked inside.

"Harlem, you came," she said as she stood up and walked toward me.

"Oh, so now you know who the fuck I am?"

"I'm sorry, but I can explain everything. I've been leaving messages on your girlfriend's phone, but she hasn't called back. I wasn't even sure that she would give you the messages. I'm so glad you came. Please help him."

"What? I don't know what you're talking about, but I didn't get any messages. I came here to confront you and ask you what the fuck happened all those years ago? Why did you let me believe you were dead for almost four fucking years and then show back up in my city and think I'd never know? And who the fuck do you want me to help? 'Cuz it better not be that old ass father of yours. That motherfucker can suck my dick!" I snapped.

"When I woke up from the coma, the doctors had me in after being shot, I had amnesia, and I couldn't remember anything of my life before the accident. Until the day I saw you a few months ago, I didn't even know who Mya was. Since the day I woke up, everything I've been told has been lies concocted by my parents. I finally got the courage to ask my father what happened, but he continued the same tired old lie that he and my mom have stuck to these last four years. So, I started to look into it myself, and memories started coming back to me when I did. Every flashback I've had of my life before, you were there. They told me my boyfriend was killed the night I got shot. They've led me to believe that you were dead all this time."

"None of this adds up. How did you know about me if you didn't remember anything about your life?" I asked, now feeling even more confused.

Mya stepped to the side. And that's when I noticed the boy lying in bed.

"Because when I woke up, the nurse informed me that I was pregnant. Hudson is my miracle baby, but now he needs a miracle. He's sick Harlem, and he has a rare blood type. It doesn't match mine, but it could match his dad's. Please, Harlem, you've got to help him. You've got to help our son..."

To Be Continued

WANT TO BE A PART OF THE GRAND PENZ FAMILY?

To submit your manuscript to Grand Penz Publications,
please send the first three chapters and synopsis to
grandpenzpublications@gmail.com